He held her close against his lean body. His kisses demanded more, and a heady fire swept through them both. "My adorable, adorable widow. I have thought of nothing else for days. You have haunted me night and day. Say you will be mine."

"Oh, yes, Wentworth. I cannot refuse you." She pulled away. "We will have to postpone our announcement. I cannot seem to rush into marriage so soon after your nephew's death."

Marriage. He stepped back and dropped his hands.

"You look thunderstruck, my lord."

"I am. I had not thought to wed again and considered you a widow. . . ."

"And therefore just anxious for your attentions. . . !"

Also by Roberta Eckert
Published by Fawcett Books:

SCANDALOUS JOURNEY

AN INDISCREET OFFER

Roberta Eckert

FAWCETT CREST • NEW YORK

A Fawcett Crest Book
Published by Ballantine Books
Copyright © 1993 by Roberta Eckert

Library of Congress Catalog Card Number: 93-90090

ISBN 0-449-22180-6

Manufactured in the United States of America

First Edition: July 1993

To Christian
with love and admiration

One

Thank God, the ordeal was almost over! They had buried Simon Wharton today and Claire knew of no one who mourned her mean-spirited stepfather's passing—least of all, she and Phoebe. What an ugly thought, she chided herself, one should think kindly of the dead. Claire frowned and twisted her handkerchief. It would not be long before the last guests left.

She glanced toward Aunt Phoebe, who read her thoughts and responded with a tight, sympathetic smile. Claire gave a slight nod of understanding. They both knew tomorrow's problems loomed larger than today's, and that thought reflected in their eyes.

Claire rose to escort the vicar and his wife to the door. Thank heavens, they were among the last of the mourners to leave. She was grateful for everyone's support, but now she needed quiet and time to think about the future.

"I will look in on you tomorrow. Call on me for any little service I can give. Claire, you have always been a favorite of mine. Look now to the future; you deserve a bright one."

"Yes, of course, and thank you, Vicar and Mrs. Harding, for your kindness," Claire said, leaning to receive a kiss on her cheek from the plump, rosy vicar's wife.

She stood and waved them good-bye as they headed down the walk. Turning, she found Squire Bradley, the last remaining guest, about to take his leave. He had apparently lingered so as to speak privately with her. A frown flitted across Claire's pale face. It was inevitable that he would try to press his suit, and at this moment she did not have enough energy left to evade him.

"My dear Miss Darington, I wish, once again, to declare my sympathy and concern," the squire said, involuntarily glancing around at the shabby condition of the room. Dismay showed on his face. He was unaware of his action and that she was reading his thoughts. Since they mirrored hers, it was not surprising she read them so readily and was not in the least offended. She knew their situation far better than he did.

"May I call upon you later in the week? You must be aware of my feelings, and I wish to put forth an offer. However, I am not without understanding of the delicacy of the timing. I would not wish to intrude on your grief. May I call next week?" he asked, waiting expectantly for her response.

A weariness trailed slowly down her body, and she nodded her head. "I am grateful for your . . . er

2

... delicacy at this time. I can barely think about my future."

"That is exactly my sentiment. I shall ride over next Tuesday, if that is agreeable," he said, with the faulty but unshakable knowledge that his presence would be welcomed. He squared his broad shoulders and pulled in his considerable midriff in hopes of presenting himself in a favorable light. He bowed over her hand, giving it a little personal squeeze, and then bid his farewell.

A sinking shiver ran down Claire's back at the moist pressure of his lips and fleshy hand. Although she nodded feebly at his remarks, her mind was simply not listening. She was only too glad to close the door to him and turn to the quiet of the house.

She leaned against the door in utter exhaustion, seemingly to gather strength that was not forthcoming. Pushing away from the door, she headed for the parlor as Aunt Phoebe bustled in with fresh, hot tea.

"Just the thing, my dear. I always say: a hot cup of tea can set the world right." Phoebe placed the tray on the small table and poured a cup, fixing it to the very well known preferences of her dear, darling niece. Any small comfort she might provide now was merely a momentary diversion, but any diversion would do.

"I am beyond tired," Claire said, gratefully taking the proffered cup and sinking into a chair.

Tea had been a scarce item because her now deceased and lately buried stepfather had considered its frequent consumption an extravagance.

"Hmm . . . heavenly, Phoebe. Tea does warm one to the very marrow."

They sipped in silence and pure enjoyment. A fire burned in the hearth, giving warmth to the chill of the dark April day. The room was a comfortable haven, and they sat in harmony, mutual affection, and support. The future hovered menacingly, but for a moment the security of hot, fresh tea and no mention of tomorrow held that fact at bay.

Finally Claire asked, "Phoebe, what is to become of us?"

"I cannot imagine. Tomorrow things will seem clearer. Everyone has been most kind. We can live for days on the food sent over during the wake. The neighbors have sent all manner of food, including hams, bread, and cheese. Our larder is fairly bursting. A sight not seen in recent times, I assure you."

"I wasn't referring to that. Although, of course, I am grateful, for it does take away the immediate worry of the next meal," Claire said. She gave a wry smile.

"I know what you meant, dear. Do you suppose Simon had some money stashed among his belongings? I know it couldn't be much; nevertheless, we ought to go through his desk and chests."

Claire stiffened. Somehow the presence of her stepfather still seemed to permeate the rooms in the same ominous measure in death as it had done in life. "I am almost too frightened to look. I would

4

feel as if I was sneaking about and somehow he would materialize in all his fury."

Phoebe's eyes widened at the envisioned scene, and she nodded in total agreement. "I am not one to speak poorly of the dead, but he was a hard man."

Claire rolled her eyes to heaven. "That is the understatement of the year, my dear Aunt Phoebe."

Phoebe's blue eyes reflected a twinkle of appreciation. "Tomorrow we can go through his papers. Claire, it has to be done. Then we will know."

"That is what I am afraid of. We will know we are destitute. Will it be service in some manor house or do I accept Squire Bradley?"

"I would sell my body in Covent Garden before I would marry Squire Bradley, and I am an old lady!"

"Aunt Phoebe! You are scandalous!" Claire said, dissolving into laughter, but mostly in release of pent-up tension.

"Well, I am glad I said it, for that is the first time I have seen you laugh in weeks. Besides, you must admit Squire Bradley is a pompous toad."

"Aunt Phoebe, you amaze me with your frankness. I have never heard you say more than a peep."

"Simon isn't here to inhibit me," she said, and primly took a sip of tea. She resisted the impulse to look around and make sure what she said was still so.

"Aunt Phoebe, is it wicked to be glad someone is ... dead?"

"Not someone like Simon. The world is better off without him. We certainly are!"

"I wonder," Claire said.

"Claire, the vicar, a man of God, was hard-pressed to find something good to say about Simon during his eulogy! I know of no single act of kindness discharged by Simon."

"I never saw any. He did see to his own comfort. If he had cared for food, we would have eaten more than oatmeal. I wonder at his destination. I suspect he is neither suffering from the cold nor among the heavenly hosts."

Phoebe laughed. "You are correct. I doubt Simon ever gave a groat to the church in his life. He was always in arrears on his pew fees. If it weren't for the fact he thought we needed to go to church to improve our various imperfections, I doubt he would ever have paid them. Simon always felt he had the corner on virtue and no amount of sermonizing could improve him."

"He found fault with everyone and everything. What kind of life is that?"

"If it had not been for you, there would have been no callers at all," Phoebe said.

"One wonders how my mother could have married him," Claire said.

"Oh, you would not have recognized him then. A charming man as you could ever meet and handsome as a Greek god, but then he was bent on having your mother."

"You are bamming me! Simon?"

"It was all designed to win your mother and her money. He swept her off her feet. She had been so lonely after your father's death."

"Then I shall avoid charming, handsome men. However, since I am quite firmly placed on the shelf, it is highly unlikely that it is something with which I shall have to contend. Squire Bradley's offer is the only one I am likely to receive."

"That is one sin I shall never forgive Simon for! He kept you from ever meeting anyone suitable. It was odd, he did approve of the squire."

"Simon liked having free servants, and since he was obligated to feed us, we fit nicely into that function."

"Aye, and he let everyone think he was kindly doing his duty to his kin by marriage only." Phoebe wrinkled her nose at the memory of the self-righteous tyrant.

"Why do you suppose he was so set on Squire Bradley?" Claire asked.

"I suspect Bradley requested no dowry. Would not surprise me one whit if he had agreed to pay Simon for his blessings," Phoebe said with disgust.

"You think so? Hmm. Well, I am lucky I have been in my majority these many years and flatly refused to accept the squire. You'd think he would give up. There are half a dozen younger ladies whom he could choose. Ladies with dowries. Phoebe, does it not strike you as really odd?"

"Perhaps you underrate your charm, but it is not surprising you do. My dear, you are a lovely, loving young woman. Had you had the opportunity of a London Season, you would have been a belle Incomparable. You are young still, and life may hold all you could desire."

"Oh, Phoebe, you dear. I am eight and twenty! My future lies in some governess position, except I am not qualified. I am little more than literate. I can run a house, but that is all."

Tears filled Phoebe's eyes as she looked at her fair niece. True, Claire looked drawn and pale, but she was comely. A fine wife she would make. There were few men alive who would deserve her. A pity— no, it was a crime! Simon should have been horse-whipped before he expired.

"Claire, we do not yet know what life has in store. Perhaps you will meet a widower."

"Why is it women always have to depend on men? They have set the world to suit themselves. It simply is not fair. I wish I were a man!" Claire exclaimed.

Phoebe nodded. "I have often wondered at the 'fairness' of life. It never seems very even to me. One sees the most undeserving people prosper."

"Phoebe, I believe it has something to do with seizing the moment or opportunity. Somehow we must make our way on our own. We are going to have to strike out and do something!"

"Great heavens, what? Whatever could we do?" Phoebe asked, with an unexplained, growing apprehension.

"Believe me, I do not know. The least will be my taking a position, but perhaps we could think of something else. Find a moment to seize."

"I quite agree, dear," Phoebe said, with the hopes of ending this direction of thought. She did not want some wild idea to pop into her niece's head. "I suggest we try not to dwell on our problems this evening. Tomorrow we will search Simon's belongings for money. We have had enough for today. Put it aside for now, Claire."

Claire looked into the worried eyes of her sweet, helpless aunt. It would be best not to continue this conversation. They both knew the problem. Phoebe was distressed enough.

"You are correct. Tomorrow we will be in better spirits to tackle our future."

$\mathcal{T}$wo

Claire rose early as usual, but she felt refreshed. The lassitude of yesterday was gone. She moved aside the curtain of the diamond-paned window. Gazing out onto a beautiful spring morning, she thought, Perhaps such beauty is an omen for better times to come. A glimmer of hope stirred in her.

The garden was a riot of early primroses, daffodils, and lilacs just beginning to open. Gardening was her one true love, and the beauty filled her with elation. It would be a pleasure to sit in it later without the fear of her uncle's voice issuing a decree to some perceived need or lack to his comfort.

The knowledge her day would be without rancor, insult, or harsh words brought an exhilaration that she thought was surely akin to being able to fly. She smiled at her comparison, but it was not far from the truth. She did feel free enough to fly away—if only she could.

What wicked thoughts! One must not think badly of the dead, she chided herself, and turned from the window. There was more than enough work to keep her mind from troubling thoughts.

Moving to the mirror, she tied her honey-colored hair into a neat bun at the nape of her neck. Her hair was thick and unruly, and before many hours passed, wayward tendrils would trail along her cheek.

She shrugged. At least it no longer made a difference, since she had only herself to please. That was freedom! She would enjoy the freedom of their situation while it lasted. It could not continue long. She would eventually have to take a position as a governess or companion, since she would not accept Squire Bradley's inevitable proposal of marriage.

It would not be his first, but she would see that it was his last. Simon had approved of the possible match, and it was sheer will that had kept her from those bonds—*her* will. Simon was no longer among the living to insist she accept Bradley.

She had paid dearly for that first refusal, but not even Simon's wrath could make her marry where her heart refused to go. Now that Simon was gone, she had only the squire to deal with, and surely he lacked any real hope that she would accept him.

Although she had long been a spinster and was unlikely to receive another offer, she would remain her own person. Having endured the harsh dictates of her stepfather, she vowed never, never to fall under the power of another man. Spinsterhood was infinitely preferable. She shrugged in a Gallic manner that suggested "so be it" and headed toward the kitchen to start breakfast.

Phoebe joined her directly, and the two women bustled about the kitchen in happy harmony. The simple task of working together unfettered was pure bliss. Phoebe, despite her years, giggled like a girl, for she, too, felt the joy of release from tyranny.

"Fresh biscuits and ham with blackberry jam. A meal fit for a king," Phoebe said with delight. "Fresh tea—and no Simon. I propose we have the remains of the rabbit stew with biscuits at noontime. I'll make us a custard. How does that sound?"

"Grand. We shall both get fat," Claire teased, knowing each could use a little plumping up. They were little more than scarecrows.

Phoebe paused and looked at Claire with a pang that was a frequent companion whenever she considered her beloved niece. There she stood in a faded brown gown, hair pulled back like a scullery maid's. Deep shadows showed beneath her beautiful eyes. It did not seem fair that this beautiful young woman had been denied a chance to make a decent match.

Claire had many attributes besides a kindly heart and an indomitable wit. She was comely, indeed, with her slender, graceful figure and a perfectly charming face. Her truly beautiful brown eyes, so lavishly flecked with gold, danced with a ready humor. And when she laughed, a tiny dimple by the side of her mouth would appear and then disappear with intriguing caprice.

Yes, Claire was lovely despite the drab, serviceable gown, but what was to become of her—them, for that matter? If only her small portion were enough to situate them in a small cottage. Phoebe looked around at the huge kitchen with its many needed repairs. They could not stay here.

"Claire, you own this house and land. You could sell it and we might have enough to get a wee cottage and live comfortably. . . ."

Thunder struck, and they stood staring at each other. The silence was deafening. Why had they not considered that before? How stupid!

"I wonder! The land is valuable. The manor would take a veritable fortune to bring it to what it had once been. 'Tis a shame, too, for it's a beautiful house."

"*Was*, my dear, was. We could never maintain it. If the land was worked, it might be profitable, but the house is beyond our means. Perhaps there is someone wanting such a place. A wealthy merchant might wish to enjoy the fruits of his profits in a fine house," Phoebe suggested, with growing optimism.

"Phoebe, I think you've hit upon the very thing! Imagine, not considering the value of the land! It belonged to mother, it must be mine! You're a genius!" She hugged Phoebe.

A grateful smile flooded Phoebe's face, for she had given what was obviously considered a good idea. She had spent most of her life in a secondary position, and it felt wonderful to be of help. Oh, she knew well the value her niece placed on her, but that was not the same as being called a genius!

"Let's go through Simon's papers and look for the name of his man of business. He must have one. We can write to him and see about selling the

manor. I do wonder how much it might fetch."
Claire's voice gained an excited pitch. "I have never
considered such a thing. Phoebe, you are right. It
might just do."

Later that morning they began their quest in Simon's room. Claire shuddered when they first entered, for it still held the aura of the dying. Those
were long, difficult days and nights she had spent
in caring for him. The task had grown more difficult with each passing day because he had become
even more demanding and ill-tempered in his ter-
minal illness. She would close this room for good
when possible.

They first searched his dresser drawers for his
key ring and squealed with triumph when they
found it. But as they made their way downstairs,
Claire fingered the keys with mounting anxiety.
She realized she was actually frightened of entering his study. Years of conditioning by intimidation
had left a terrifying apprehension of crossing that
threshold. Her steps faltered at the door of his
study. They paused at the door and stood frozen, unable to continue.

"Do it," Phoebe whispered. Why she whispered,
she could not imagine. No one else was there.

"It's like he's haunting us—as if he will leap out
and start yelling. Don't you feel it?" Claire whispered back.

"Of course, but open the door. The man is dead!"

"Why are we whispering?"

".Good heavens, I don't know."

Claire took a breath, but her fingers continued to tremble as she tried each key. They heard the click and froze again. Claire remained paralyzed as her heart pounded and a cold sweat broke out along her brow. She glanced toward Phoebe, whose lace cap sat askew over a face with eyes as large as saucers. Claire could not repress a smile and then a giggle born in the expectant expression on Phoebe's face. It broke the tension.

Claire turned the knob, flung open the door, and boldly stepped into the room. All the draperies were closed, leaving the room in semidarkness. The shadows gave an eerie atmosphere. She crossed the floor and pulled back the draperies. Light flooded the room. Dust was everywhere, and cobwebs hung in the corners. The room had not been thoroughly cleaned in years. It looked as though Simon had just dusted a place to sit at the desk. At that moment Claire knew Simon had truly been mad.

They stood amazed at the fine quality of the furniture. The good pieces in the rest of the house had been sold little by little over the years and the rooms closed one by one.

This room held all the beautiful furniture that must have belonged to her father when he died. This wasn't Simon's room; it was her father's! Simon had only been a cruel interloper. Strength rushed through her veins. By the Eternal, Claire vowed silently, Simon would not defeat her in death any more than he had defeated her in life.

"Phoebe, we have work to do if we are to find our means to adventure."

Adventure? A wee cottage in Cotswood, adventure? Phoebe cast a worried look in Claire's direction but merely said, "Yes, dear."

They continued to spend the morning going through Simon's things. His papers and ledgers were a mystery to them both. Simon seemed to have some kind of code, though each doubted they would understand ledgers written in any manner.

When they found the name of Mr. Gibbons, who was the man of business, Claire stuck the letter bearing his name and address in her apron pocket. "This is the most important piece of information. I will write him today. Pray there is not a mountain of debts to be paid."

Next, a bag of coins was found tucked back in a locked drawer, and they spent the better part of an hour counting and sorting them.

"Great Scott, there is over a hundred pounds here—all in small coins. How odd," Claire whispered when they finished.

Phoebe scoffed. "Hardly odd. He doled it out in drips and dabs so we would not ask for or expect much."

Claire leaned back on her heels with a glimmer of an idea beginning to form. "I shall write this Mr. Gibbons immediately. If Simon had these coins, there might just be more, enough for us to buy a small place. Brighton, perhaps."

Aunt Phoebe clapped her hands. "It would be a dream come true. Maybe you could find a widower."

"Phoebe, no more of that! I have no intentions of

marrying. You must promise me you will not make that suggestion again. Between Simon and Squire Bradley, I find I have no desire to be under the commands of some man who thinks he is born to rule women. No, thank you, and that is final!"

Poor Phoebe, who always aimed to please, felt her lower lip tremble. "I am sorry, dear. You must credit my thoughts to the expectations of the society that I have always known."

"Phoebe, how can you say that? You have remained single."

"It was not by choice. Believe me, for years it was 'Poor Phoebe, she never married, you know.' A spinster is an object of pity, and it is not pleasant."

"Oh, I *am* sorry. I never even considered that. I spoke unthinkingly. You have always been a source of joy and comfort to me. I shudder to think of what my life would have been without you."

"I know, dear, no need to worry about saying anything to offend. It is a simple truth. Spinsters always end up as poor relations, performing tasks of a servant or governess. The only privilege they receive is being allowed to take meals at the family table." Phoebe scoffed, but pain was easily heard in her voice.

"Phoebe, you amaze me. I always thought you managed very well. I never thought it bothered you," Claire said in utter amazement. How little we consider others, she chided herself. Imagine never knowing that about her aunt, who had acted like a mother to her all these years. Claire blushed.

"I did not mind while your mother was alive, but

Simon never let me forget the burden I placed upon him." Tears filled the pretty blue eyes of her aunt.

Claire reached out and hugged her. "Well, dear, dear Phoebe, we have each other now. We shall do quite well together."

Phoebe wiped away a trailing tear. "Believe me, it is far better to be a widow. One has ever so much more freedom!"

"Really? I have never thought of that either. I am beginning to wonder what I did think about. But you are right. A widow has respect and sympathy. Society does not frown when she lives in an establishment of her own."

Phoebe nodded and repeated, "A spinster is an object of pity." She sniffed away a tear.

"Widow," Claire repeated, with sly merriment in her eyes.

Three

Squire Bradley was considered by some if not handsome, at least a man of distinction. While not yet running to fat, he was beginning to acquire a "prosperous middle-aged" girth. He was not yet forty. His hair had begun to thin and he combed it intricately in a feeble effort to hide his pending baldness.

Claire disdained this obvious sign of vanity. In fact, she disdained much in the man that would have gone unnoticed in another. She held little charity for him with nary a qualm at the harshness of her judgment. All too often Bradley had conspired with Simon concerning her future, and she was not about to overlook it now. He had worked behind her back to seek Simon's approval of their marriage.

She was not sure whether it was she or the land that he desired. It made no difference. She could not be offended at either, since she would see he obtained neither. It was now in her power to refuse him once and for all.

Watching him cross the room, she stiffened her

19

spine to sit a little taller and more primly. Without Simon to bully her, she felt stronger and showed it in her bearing. Again she vowed not to succumb to his tedious entreaties. No matter how bleak her future, marrying him would be too much of a sacrifice. The thought of his marriage bed and his pawing hands was enough to make her remain a virgin forever. She suppressed a shudder.

He had taken care to present himself to advantage, and she could not fault his appearance. Still, she read in his countenance an insincerity; it had always been so. He revealed only the surface of his personality. That was offensive enough. She could only hazard a guess at his true self, and it was not a pretty thought.

She knew better than to expect a romantic man, for such existed only in novels. But her feelings went beyond that. There was an underlying quality that made her distrust him. She wondered if it was selfishness with a hidden streak of malice that she sensed. Often she thought she glimpsed a cruel curl to his lips while a similar light glinted across his eyes. He would be spouting the most prosaic or flowery comment when she perceived this phenomenon. This insight was so strong, it disturbed her, and she had always tried to keep her distance.

Often she wondered if it was only in her imagination because he had always been in league with Simon. That alone condemned the man in her eyes. She was not going to test the validity of her suspicion today; she was far too weary from worry.

"My dear Claire," he began, "I hope I find you in

good health." There was concern in his voice and a pious smile on his lips.

The image of a spider with a fly caught in his web came to mind. She watched his eyes trail down her face and linger on her bosom.

"Do sit, Squire Bradley. May I bring your attention to some tea?"

He was brought up by the sharpness of her voice and the disapproval in her eyes. Realizing he had been careless in his drifting gaze, he offered an innocuous smile. To hell with it, he thought, he had carried a desire for her far too long without being satisfied. He would have her soon, and on his terms.

He dismissed his prurient thoughts with the merest shrug. It was easy; all he had to do was think of her land. He wanted that far more than her tempting body. Besides, he never had any problem in finding those willing to answer his needs.

He seated himself and again took in her appearance. Pale purple rings marked her eyes; her skin was finely drawn and as fragile-looking as delicate porcelain. He perceived her attitude. She looked cold and prim, and he suddenly doubted her warmth in bed. Lord, how he hated pious women. The desire to bend her to his will crept into his mind. She had always remained aloof, even haughty, and it rankled. Well, she needed him now. He had the upper hand.

A bright smile appeared in a face carrying calculating eyes. "I am delighted to see you so well. I know the sudden death of your stepfather is a great sorrow for you, and I was concerned for you."

21

"Indeed? His health had been poor for some time."

"Aye. Sad to say, but that it was," Bradley answered mildly, suddenly finding himself wary.

"You need not concern yourself with us, Squire Bradley. Aunt Phoebe and I shall manage."

"That is why I have come. Perhaps too prematurely, but I feel it my duty to speak in hopes of lifting some of your worry. You know I have . . . er . . . been an admirer of yours for . . . er . . . some time. I always thought that Simon, while professing friendship, actually stood in my way of winning you. I want you to consider the advantages of being my wife."

"Advantages?"

Squire Bradley squirmed. She was not dull-witted; why was she acting as if she did not understand?

"You need protecting. You simply cannot remain here alone. You must marry me."

"Must? I have Aunt Phoebe's welfare to consider, and I quite agree we cannot remain here."

"My house is big enough for you and your aunt. It would be the ideal arrangement. Our lands march side by side. I can turn this land into a profit. You will lack for nothing. I am not like Simon, for I would see you properly dressed."

Claire was amazed at his frankness. She was also surprised at his remarking on Simon's penurious ways. "You are very kind to show such interest. I am flattered by your offer of marriage. I know you mean well by me, but I cannot marry you."

"Cannot or will not?"

"They are one and the same."

He jumped to his feet. "You cannot refuse me! How will you survive?"

"I shall sell the land."

"Sell the land? You cannot! You must marry me. Simon wanted the marriage." He was wild with anger, and his voice carried incredulity.

Claire was taken aback by his outburst. She was utterly naive as to the ways of the world, especially the ways of men. However, she was no girl, and the years spent in cajoling her curmudgeonly stepfather had taught her the wisdom of discretion. She had spoken far too plainly.

A warning signaled in her mind as a little shiver raised the hackles on her neck. She perceived a vague danger in the squire. He had overplayed his argument by suggesting she was unprotected. If he so coveted her land, might he not force her into some . . . She could not finish the thought.

"Oh, you misunderstand me, Squire Bradley," she lied. "I am most appreciative of your concern." She offered a rare and dazzling smile.

He stopped in midsentence, stunned by the beauty of her sudden smile. He was momentarily struck silent.

"You must make allowances for my grief," she continued, with the easy skill of appeasing and wheedling she had learned at Simon's side. She fluttered her eyes and smiled wistfully, and she hated herself for doing so. If she were a man, she could tell him to go to hades before she planted a facer on him. Women had to play false in order to survive. If it was ever in her power, she would change that!

"Please be seated and let me offer you some tea. You cannot expect me to be as practical as you at this difficult time. Let us put aside, only temporarily, I assure you, your kind offer. I shall consider it in the most favorable light, but it is not seemly for me to do so . . . so soon . . . after. Simon is not gone to his grave a week yet."

Squire Bradley was mollified by her words. He had been too precipitous. He would wait.

"You are correct. It would not do for us to make such an announcement before a proper mourning period. Keep in mind I have only your welfare at heart." He spoke as he rose and prepared to leave. "I shall look in on you soon. You must not sell the land, Claire," the squire said just as he departed.

She perceived it a warning and returned a smile. "No, I shall do nothing hasty. I promise. I shall consult you before any such step."

Bradley smiled with satisfaction as he placed his hat on his head and departed.

She was relieved to see him leave. The man was persistent beyond belief! The house might be falling around her head, but it was Squire Bradley who would drive her from the vicinity. If only she would hear back from Simon's man of business soon.

Aunt Phoebe poked her head around the door. "Has he gone?"

"Aye, and I hate myself for the lies I gave him. Why should I have to lie just to hold him at bay?" Claire threw out her arms in disgust.

"That bad, eh?" Phoebe asked.

"Worse. He pressed his suit. I had to feign grief for Simon, which is wholly hypocritical. He actually *warned* me of my vulnerability. The worst part was that he meant it. He makes me shiver."

"Oh, my. Perhaps that Mr. Gibbons will answer your letter soon and we will be able to sell this land."

"Oh, Aunt Phoebe, I hope so!"

Spring rain pelted the windows, forcing Phoebe and Claire to scurry around placing containers under the various leaks. The sound of the pinging drops as they hit the buckets would drive a saint to drink, and Claire was no saint.

Phoebe watched her niece pace back and forth. The waiting, the indecision, the unknown, and the inactivity were making Claire all sixes and sevens. Poor Claire, Phoebe thought, wishing she could do something. An idea came to mind.

"Claire, dear. I have been thinking. Perhaps we should go through your mother's old trunks. There might be information or deeds to this land there."

Claire stopped in her relentless tracks. "Aunt Phoebe, what would I do without you? Why didn't I think of that? I swear, it's a good thing I have you. It seems I am bogged down in the problem and not the solution. Now, where are her trunks?"

Phoebe beamed with delight. It was wonderful the way Claire made her feel so useful. Maybe she was. "I have no idea, but surely somewhere in the attic?"

Claire's restlessness disappeared immediately, and it was only minutes before she and Phoebe, armed with candles, made their way to the attic. The room was enormous, and they hardly knew where to begin their search.

They opened one trunk covered with dust but bearing her mother's initials. "Oh, look at these gowns. They must have been Mother's. The fabrics, the workmanship—Phoebe, they were beautiful! I am glad she had them."

Phoebe smiled. "She was the catch of her Season, and your father loved her very much. Such a pity he died so young." Phoebe fought back tears at the memory of the sister she had loved.

"How could she have married Simon, after knowing my father?" Claire hissed.

"I told you. She was lonely. Remember, she had been happily married and had no reason to believe she would not be so again. The pity was, Simon never measured up to your father. I think that was what turned him so mean."

"Look at the beautiful fabrics. Phoebe, this black bombazine gown, it has yards and yards of fabric. Why not make something for us?"

"We could. There is more than enough, with the slender skirts of today."

"Look at the laces and braids. Phoebe, would it be wrong for us to fashion a few gowns out of these fabrics?"

"Great Scott, no. What better use? Let's do it. There is no Simon to stop us."

They spent the next several days cutting and

stitching. Phoebe was grateful for the diversion. Claire's outlook brightened as she threw herself into the task of making them each a dress. In fact, Phoebe kept Claire as busy as possible while they waited to hear from Mr. Gibbons, the man of business.

$\mathcal{F}our$

$\mathcal{M}$r. Thaddeous Gibbons was punctual, arriving precisely at ten o'clock, as agreed upon by letter from Miss Darington. He checked his pocket watch, then pulled the bell chain at the front entrance. The door bell echoed the ten o'clock chimes of the stately hall clock.

Claire and Phoebe had lived every day with this event in mind. They had been anxious, nervous, and impatient for Mr. Gibbons's arrival since dawn. Phoebe prayed for enough money from the sale of Rosehill to survive modestly without worry. Claire prayed for freedom from her drab, disheartening life and a little excitement before she was too old.

"It's about time," Phoebe muttered at the sound of the bell, and she straightened her lace cap as Claire hurried to answer the door.

Having found, during his many years in business, that social intercourse between himself and his clients was not advisable, Mr. Gibbons had taken a room at the Kings Arms. When his work was finished or he reached an impasse, he could merely excuse himself and be neither beholden nor captive to his clients' opinions.

It was far better to keep his relationship on a professional basis. It was not in his makeup to advise on money matters, then sit through a dinner of chitchat. He had learned from Miss Darington's letter that the family was in mourning for the death of Miss Darington's stepfather. Still, he was more than a little curious to meet his wealthy client, since he had never seen or communicated with her. He had always considered it most unusual, but then he had always thought Simon Wharton a bit odd.

He had seen to Miss Darington's estate. In actuality, it was administered by default. Miss Darington had never spent a penny of her mother's inheritance, and the money had grown with interest for twenty years. She was a very wealthy lady indeed, and he was curious to meet her. He had always suspected that the reason he had never had contact with her was that she might be mentally deficient. A fact her stepfather might keep confidential, which would explain the circumstances of the untouched legacy.

Mr. Gibbons did not miss the dilapidated condition of the once fine house, and it astonished him. His vow of remaining detached from the personal lives of his clients wavered. Why had they allowed the house to deteriorate? Very strange indeed. In fact, it made him uncomfortable. He was glad to be staying at the Kings Arms, for it would appear there was little in the way of amenities to be found in these forlorn surroundings.

To his surprise, the door was opened by a young and exceedingly attractive lady. She was dressed in mourning and kindly asked him to enter. He noted her elegant carriage and soft, pleasing voice. Instantly he knew her identity, for she was the image of her mother.

Gibbons had a sinking feeling all was not as it should be. He had admired her mother, a feeling that far exceeded what he could say about her second husband, Simon Wharton.

"I am Miss Darington. Please come in." She stood aside and allowed him passage. He removed his hat and stepped inside the large foyer.

The hall fared little better than the exterior, with its peeling paint, but a beautiful bouquet of flowers sat on a freshly beeswaxed table. It proclaimed a civility despite poverty. The house was both shabby and spotless. How odd, how very odd, he thought, knowing the fortune at hand.

He glanced at the young lady in dismay and felt a flush of embarrassment at the flicker of apology in her eyes. She was ashamed of the condition of the house; it was obvious, although the words were never spoken. His curiosity grew.

With an unaccustomed pang of sympathy, he followed the slender young lady into a study at the end of the hall. She offered a polite hope his trip had been agreeable. She seemed perfectly normal to him; no mental lack was evident, and the mystery deepened.

Mr. Gibbons was perplexed by the first-rate interior of the study, for it was in total contrast to what he had previously seen. He struggled to hide his bewilderment.

He had long ago learned to mask facial expressions that might give away his thoughts. It was imperative in his business, for in dealing with the aristocracy one did not allow oneself to show disapproval. He had found a universal belief among the wealthy that they were inevitably correct in most matters.

"Mr. Gibbons, may I present my aunt, Miss Greene."

They exchanged greetings, and he refused the chair indicated to him. "We have much to go over. I suggest we use the desk," he said. "This is all rather confidential; do you want to begin immediately?" He glanced toward Miss Greene, not knowing if she was to remain during their discussion.

"I shall see to some refreshments," Phoebe said. She rose and left the room before Claire could insist she remain.

Mr. Gibbons efficiently began removing vast sheaves of papers and documents. Claire watched the thin, austere-looking man with growing apprehension. What were all these papers, and what in heaven's name did they all mean? Pray God there were no mortgages to be paid off, she thought.

His movements were reflected in the economy of his speech and modest dress. His pragmatic demeanor began to offer a glimmer of confidence to Claire.

Would she even understand the business matters contained in all these papers? She crossed the worn Tabiz carpet and drew up a chair next to the desk. Waiting silently, as he arranged his papers, she began to twist at the handkerchief she was carrying. Where could they go? By what means could she take care of Phoebe and herself? Her mouth became dry, her head began to pound, and her face became as pale as chalk.

"As you are aware, your fortune is vast. You have not availed yourself of any monies, and it has grown into an enormous sum. I assume your stepfather kept you informed and provided for you himself so that you had no need to touch your funds."

The word *enormous* staggered her. She had an enormous fortune? The words buzzed in her brain. For a split second she thought she might faint. She clutched the arms of her chair to steady herself. "No, I am totally unaware of my situation," she answered feebly, her words barely above a whisper.

Mr. Gibbons looked up from his papers and broke his rule by offering an equally surprised expression. He muttered, "I see." But he did not.

Silence dominated the room for several seconds. "Then it is best we begin at the beginning." He wondered at the circumstances that would allow a young lady to have no knowledge of her monetary worth and live in obviously genteel poverty.

They spent the next several hours huddled together over pages of ledgers. His voice droned on as he went over each and every investment. Phoebe brought in hot tea twice and they barely noticed her, so intent were they in the subject at hand.

At last they finished. Mr. Gibbons sat back and allowed a sigh to escape. He removed his spectacles and began to gather up the papers. "I hope this brings you a more ... er ... normal existence. I feel somehow guilty that I have never contacted you. But your stepfather seemed very rational and allowed your holdings to grow. I step in only when I see guardians depleting a legacy and am very glad when they do not."

"I quite understand. You need not fault yourself. I am overwhelmed. My mind is unable to grasp the idea that I am comfortably well-off."

"Not well-off, Miss Darington, but exceedingly wealthy."

She nodded, still in shock.

"If you will be so kind as to see me out. I wish to return to London as soon as possible."

Claire walked him to the front door and bid him good day.

"Now, remember, I am arranging for any transfer of funds you might need. Please inform me of the quarterly sum you desire. I suggest you make the necessary repairs on the house. If you decide to sell, it must have a sound roof. I also suggest you not rush into any decisions of selling Rosehill. Wait until you know how and where you wish to live. You must feel free to call upon me anytime. I wish you happiness. Do come to London; you would like it, I am convinced."

As soon as he had gone, Claire picked up her

skirts and ran as fast as she could to the back of the house. She knew she would find Aunt Phoebe in the kitchen.

"I am rich! Filthy rich, disgustingly rich. Aunt Phoebe, we can go to London or anywhere in the world we might wish!" She grabbed Phoebe and danced around the vast room, hugging her while laughing and crying at the same time.

"Rich?" Phoebe managed between twirls. "Stop it, child. You leave me quite breathless!"

Twilight was fading and night shadows began taking over their world with creeping shades of indigo. The spring night was chilly, and the two ladies huddled near the hearth in hushed tones of conversation. They had spent the entire afternoon discussing the change in their circumstances.

"Phoebe, we are going to enjoy ourselves. The first thing I shall purchase is a carriage and horse."

"You'll need a coachman and grooms," Phoebe said, still clinging to the notion that unnecessary expenses must be avoided.

"Of course. We shall also hire household servants and a lady's maid. Oh, Phoebe, look at my hands from all the household work. They are so red and rough. And look at my nails. They're a mess! It will take a year to get them to look like a lady of leisure's."

"We are hardly ladies of fashion. Do we wish to be?"

"Of course. I shall be the most fashionable lady ever to grace London! What fun! How very, very

nuch fun. We will cut a dash unlike any London
ras ever seen."

"My dear, I am quite beyond the 'cutting a dash'
ige, but I shall enjoy watching you do so." Phoebe
:huckled.

"Well, you shall be a very elegant matron."

"I am a spinster, and airs do not please me."

The little censure rolled past Claire, who was in
a state of euphoria. No practical reality had yet
reached her mind.

"Claire, you are too old to go to London for a Season. It will be proper for us to go and set up a household, but we will still be single ladies beyond the
first bloom of youth. Me, more beyond—by two de-
cades, to be sure." She laughed.

Claire smiled. "You are right. I must look at this
more practically. We know we have all the money
we want. We can buy pretty clothes and smart carriages and meet members of society. Surely we can
entertain?" Claire asked, beginning to see the lim-
its of their situation. She was too old to have a
come-out and too young to dash about without censure. She was a single, maiden lady and firmly on
the shelf.

"My money will attract suitors," she said.

"Exactly my point. Who wants a suitor merely
after her money?"

"Never. As I have said, I do not seek a husband,
but if I did, I would want someone to love me, not
my money! Oh, how complicated all this is. One
would think having money would solve your problems, not bring more."

"I am afraid money and affairs of the heart have been the source of problems since man began his sojourn on this earthly dominion," Phoebe said in wry humor and a bit of caution.

Claire paid no heed to her aunt and continued with tumbling words and mounting joy. "We can go to London and set up a discreet household and behave in a circumspect manner. We can still have some fun!"

"A spinster cannot dash about without being considered fast, and well you know it," Phoebe warned, and began feeling as if she was offering only thoughts dampening to Claire's happiness.

"I don't care what 'they' think!"

"Do you wish to attract a man who thinks you are fast?"

"Good heavens, no."

They sat a few moments mulling over this new set of limitations. Phoebe was feeling a little guilty about her negative remarks, and Claire was trying to bring her desires into a feasible prospect.

"I've been considering what you said the other day about the freedom widows enjoy. Therefore, I have decided to become a 'widow.'" Claire watched the open-mouthed shock of her aunt and rushed on with her plans before Phoebe could object.

"After we buy a carriage and clothes and whatever else we need in London, we shall go to Bath. That's it! We shall go to Bath during my 'mourning' for my dear, departed husband. I will cream my hands every night, and by the time we go to London I'll look as if I've never worked a day in my ife." Claire's eyes twinkled with mischief and humor as she continued, to the dismay of her mute aunt.

"We will have a marvelous wardrobe made and even take dancing lessons. I can catch up on all my lacking social graces, which must count by the score. We can be ready in a year!" Claire jumped to her feet and waltzed around the room. "What a splendid scheme. It will work!"

Aunt Phoebe listened to Claire with mounting concern yet somehow became caught up in her niece's excitement. She found herself agreeing. "Yes, it can be done in Bath. Fewer questions are asked in Bath. We can meet the people necessary to make connections in society. We will need entry, my dear. You can be ready for London in style, no doubt about it. And you will take London by storm," Phoebe said, deciding she should offer her niece some enthusiasm. "But you do not have to be a widow to do all that!"

"Of course, I shall be twenty-nine by then. Oh, dear."

"The perfect age for a widow. You look twenty-two."

"You say that because you love me."

"Well, you will when you're dressed to the nines! We shall have to put an armed guard to protect you." Phoebe began to enjoy the fantasy as much as Claire.

"Phoebe, are there any distant relatives of Mother's we could call on? Perhaps well-connected friends who might give entry?"

"Family, no. But there might be those who remember your mother. I have several acquaintances we will call. But remember, I made no mark on society," Phoebe said.

"We must have everything in place before we make ourselves known to any persons you knew previously."

"Yes, the story has to be exactly set to the last detail or we shall be found out. Are you sure you want to complicate all this by pretending to be a widow?"

Claire nodded emphatically. "Who will be my dear, departed husband?"

"Well, we can't just make up a name. You will have to have some obscure family. You cannot just make up a family, for you will have to have some background. Now, if you were a French émigré, you might get away with it. I am sure that is the case with many of our émigrés. Families enhanced beyond recognition."

"Yes, you are right. How? Could I have married some third son of a family from Northumberland, or Scotland?" Claire asked.

"Yes, some obscure yet noble family. How delicious!"

"We will search for a family, small in number, distant and not inclined to society. We were married a few days before he was shipped off to the Peninsular War. How does that sound?"

"A very tragic tale, but how are you going to find a family like this?"

"Phoebe, you forget, I am rich! Money will buy

lmost anything. I will pay someone to search out
uch a family."

"Then he would know your secret. Might try
lackmail."

"Phoebe! You see flaws in everything. We have
o think positive."

"My dear, you do not want to be exposed as a fraud
1st as you manage to achieve the life you seem to
ave your heart set on. For me, I would be content
vith a nice home in the country and no worries.
3ut we must make allowances for your youth and
he fact that you have been denied all that young
adies should have."

"Is it wrong of me to want a chance to see a real
vallroom?"

"No, my dear, it is only natural. Perhaps you will
even catch a husband. With your face, figure, and
ortune you will have a choice among dozens."

"I am not in mind for a husband. Men just tell
ne what to do. I shall be my own mistress."

"You must be discreet, if that is what you have
n mind," Phoebe chided.

Claire blushed. "That is *not* what I had in mind,
and well you know it!"

Phoebe laughed softly. "I know, dear, but I sus-
bect love will find you anyway."

"Love is a lie."

"Claire, I am amazed at your admitted lack of
knowledge of the world beyond the boundaries of
Rosehill on the one hand, and your sweeping state-
ments of knowledge of love and men on the other.
Frankly, you know nothing of either."

Claire's eyes widened. "Well, I have eyes," sh
said, somewhat humbled.

"Let's hope you have some sense, too," Phoeb
added dryly, but humor shone in her eyes.

"I shan't disappoint you," Claire said.

"I did not think for a moment you would."

Five

"Claire, you simply must do something to subdue the vitality you are radiating. Your demeanor is positively indecent for one so 'recently aggrieved,' " Phoebe said. She chuckled, for in truth she was delighted with her niece's glowing countenance.

"Then perhaps on this journey to London, you should play the widow and I the companion, for I cannot stop smiling. When all our plans are settled and we go to Bath to take on our new life, then I shall become the widow. Perhaps by then I can bring my feeling of euphoria under control. Frankly, I hope not," Claire replied, with a dimpling smile.

"What if we meet someone on the way, then meet them in London or Bath?" Phoebe said, with mounting concern over the growing complexity of the deception Claire was weaving.

"Who will we meet? Innkeepers? Stableboys?" Claire asked, then shrugged. "Besides, with my mourning veil down, who would even see my face, let alone ever recognize me again?"

Phoebe nodded. "I suppose you are correct, but shall not play the widow. I am still not comfortable with your schemes. Remember, the more compli cated you make them, the more lies we shall have to recall. I have difficulty in remembering what day of the week it is. I know I shall be quite feather headed controlling a pack of lies. Why can't we be who we are?"

"Phoebe, we've gone over this before! I am far too long on the shelf. Plain and simple, I am a spinster Taking the guise of a widow will give me all the status and freedom I want. A widow is automati cally considered more worldly and worthy than a mere spinster."

Phoebe knew only too well that was so. She nod ded.

Claire continued. "Why do so many families sac rifice their daughters' happiness just to have them married off? Because society does not recognize the worth of a woman for herself; it must be through some man! Think of the many worthy women reduced to the role of nursemaid or companion— little more than servants—to family members because they have not married. And even worse, think of those who have taken husbands they could not abide, merely because they could not endure the stigma set by remaining single. Someday, let us hope, this will change, but for now it is the truth.

"With you at my side, we can have a scintillating salon. We shall set up our establishment and do as we please."

"Within reason, my dear." Phoebe arched an eyebrow.

"Well, of course. I shall not resort to loose morals, but I can be escorted about with far less scrutiny. Oh, what fun! We shall cut a dash, I tell you now."

"That is exactly my worry, dear."

"Phoebe, are you honestly thinking I shall become a madcap miss?"

"I wasn't contemplating the words *shall become*."

Claire laughed. "It will work like a charm; you'll see."

Claire turned to the passing scenery. She had never been out of Yorkshire, and the new vistas held an irresistible fascination. The day began sunny, but by the time they reached Lincolnshire the sun became covered by ever-darkening clouds. The threatening weather could not daunt her spirits, and she sat relaxed in the knowledge she had left Rosehill in good hands.

She had faith in the couple hired to oversee the property and the mending of the roof. A house with a faulty roof would be difficult to sell, so that expenditure was a wise one. The only discomforting thought was Squire Bradley, for he was counting on marriage to grab her land. She shuddered with the image of his finding out the property might go up for sale.

For now, though, she felt safe with the strapping Dalton brothers as outriders. She remembered the pleading entreaties it had taken for their mama to agree to their accompanying her. No one could out-ride, outshoot, or outfight these country lads. She and Phoebe could be no safer in a convent than with them as protectors.

She pursed her lips, hoping she could manage her promise to Mrs. Dalton to keep the boys from harm's way in the big city. Surely there would be many temptations for them, but she would keep a sharp eye on their activities. A small worry frown appeared. Each step on her way to "freedom" brought a new obligation. Was freedom an illusion? Better that than dying of boredom, she told herself.

The hired coach was poorly sprung and achingly slow, to be sure, but with each lumbering turn of the carriage wheels the distance grew. She was well away from Rosehill and Squire Bradley. Bradley would have to buy the land if he wanted it.

When it began to sprinkle, Claire worried the roads would become slower. She hoped to make the Royal Rose in Grantham before nightfall. Having written earlier to book the best rooms, she sighed contentedly with the thought that everything was well with her world.

They reached the inn well before dusk. A magnificent crested coach stood before the entrance to the inn. Servants were bustling about as though the king himself had arrived.

Will and Jamie Dalton dismounted and came to assist the ladies, the hostlers being otherwise occupied. The coachman jumped down from the box and helped the stableboys with the team.

The red-faced and portly innkeeper met them with bows and a running conversation on the honor of having them stay at his stellar inn. Although obviously preoccupied, he rattled on about the fine food and rooms prepared for their arrival. He was in a flap about something. He was sputtering and bowing in such profusion as to make himself incomprehensible.

The two ladies in mourning, flanked by two husky country lads, presented a singular sight. Claire had dropped her heavy veil and trailed behind Phoebe, who was declaring their needs to the nodding innkeeper. "We shall require the private dining room for our meal, which I hope can be served soon. Our journey has been long and tiring."

"There is a bit of a problem," he finally said, wiping his perspiring red face with his apron and shifting uncomfortably. He glanced with apprehension to see the other's reaction, but the veil hid her face.

"The Earl of Wentworth has arrived and taken the dining room. I am sure you understand my predicament. I shall arrange to have your meal served in your rooms. The privacy will suit you, considering your situation and all. I quite understand your not wanting to eat in the taproom." He finished his speech and waited, hoping for their acquiescence.

They had written and reserved the room, but how was he to know the earl would descend upon his humble inn with his entourage? The earl had never done so before, and he did not wish to offend.

Several liveried servants were busy bringing in luggage with an air of superiority. Claire and Phoebe could hardly step aside fast enough for the haute creatures moving to pass them on their way to the stairs. The ladies stood silent for a moment. Phoebe turned to Claire for direction. Claire nodded.

"Let me show you to your rooms," the proprietor said with a sigh of relief, and headed toward the stairs.

Claire turned to the boys. "Jamie and Will, take your meal in the taproom, but mind you, not too much ale. I promised your mama, and besides, we want an early start in the morning," Claire whispered to the formidable young men. Their size alone would keep them out of trouble, she thought.

They nodded happily and headed for the warmth of a fire and a good meal. The ladies followed the innkeeper up the stairs just as the sound of laughter emanated from the private dining room. She had to step aside again for the bewigged and satin-dressed footmen.

Claire pursed her lips. When they reached the upper hall, she said, "I hope you have not given our rooms to the earl, too."

The innkeeper flushed. "Well . . . I . . . you must understand . . ." He was now addressing Claire, as she seemed to be the one in charge. The older one must be a companion, he thought, hoping not to offend any more than he already had done.

He did not finish his sentence as he opened the door to a suite of two rooms. The rooms were small but they were clean, and a generous fire burned in the grate. The beds looked inviting. But Claire was becoming annoyed.

"How can you even set up a table for us to eat?"

"There is room, I assure you. I do it all the time. Most ladies prefer to eat away from the public areas," the innkeeper said, with a hidden implication in the words *most ladies*. He bowed and backed away. "I have to get back to the earl." He left and closed the door.

"My bones are weary, child. With a good meal I shall sleep like the dead," Phoebe said, removing her gloves and cloak. "Excuse my reference to the dead."

Claire's eyes were alive with the excitement of her beginning adventure. Sleep was far from her thoughts. Removing her outer cloak, she washed her hands and face. She tidied her hair and replaced her bonnet. "Why should we give way to an earl? We are free Englishwomen. Why should we be less comfortable than a fool who happened to be born a nobleman?"

Phoebe's eyes widened. A horrible, creeping apprehension entered her mind. What was Claire about? "Now, child, what difference does it make? We'll be comfortable, I'm sure."

"That's not the point! I wrote ahead, reserving the dining room and the best beds. We have the

47

money to pay. Why should we step aside for a mere earl? You are an elderly lady and I am a grieving widow. Why should we?"

"Claire, I am not elderly! Older, yes, but not elderly! And you are no grieving widow! Behave."

"Excuse me, Aunt Phoebe, I have something to attend to." Claire left the room.

Phoebe rolled her eyes. Now what?

It was but seconds before Claire was back with Will and Jamie in tow. They were grinning as wide as a country mile.

Claire directed them to take her luggage to the room at the end of the hall. She led the way and opened the door to a lovely, large room. "This is more to my liking," she said. She waved the boys in with the portmanteaus.

"Now remove these articles and trunks to the room we were previously in," she said as she crossed the room to stand by the warm and welcoming fire as if proclaiming the room hers.

The Dalton boys happily obeyed, and it was only minutes before the earl's luggage had been removed. Claire was unaware of her luck in the absence of his lordship's valet. She luckily missed a potentially vulgar scene.

Claire thanked them and sent them back to eat the meal they had ordered. "Jiss let us know anything ye be wanting," they said. And off they bounded, back to the lively taproom.

They were met at the bottom of the stairs by the previously mentioned valet and the innkeeper in a state of acute anxiety.

"Our mistress didn't like the room. We aim to see she has what she wants," they said, and shouldered their way past the men.

The innkeeper felt faint.

$\mathcal{S}$ix

$\mathcal{T}$he Earl of Wentworth, the Right Honorable Julian Alexander Anseley, second viscount and baron of Montgomery in the county of Tyrone, was seven years old when his father died in 1782. He was educated at Eton and at Christ Church, Oxford, where he earned the honorary degree of master of arts.

In 1800 Sir Julian was appointed lieutenant-colonel of the militia, and in 1803 he was elected a representative peer for Ireland and inherited the Earldom of Wentworth from one Maxwell Kent, a distant relative, with the stipulation that he assume the surname of his benefactor. The origin of this later title dates from 1673 and the archbishop of Armagh but had become extinct in 1745. When Viscount Montgomery was given the dignity of an earl, he was twenty-eight. A contemporary was quoted as saying he was the most qualified man he knew.

Few noblemen have embarked upon their career with greater advantage than Julian Anseley Kent. In reaching his majority, Sir Julian possessed a fine fortune, excellent education, and considerable talents. He was shrewd, perceptive, and intelligent. His lordship's manners, deportment, and demeanor befitted his rank and disposition.

However, the one pitfall that was probably the most unfortunate that could befall a young nobleman was the death of his father at so early an age. His mother fairly doted on him. As a result, he was courted, flattered, and acquiesced to by all those around him. His arrogance was legendary.

The loss of his father, who might have guided his steps on stricter paths and kept him warned of the evils awaiting the advantaged and inexperienced youth, was unfortunate. Without this guidance Sir Julian indulged in all the enticements available to the rich.

At thirty-four the earl was no longer inexperienced. He was a man of considerable charm, when he chose to exercise it, but he was jaded and cynical and seldom found reason to extend himself. The one exception was his daughter, Julie, whom he adored.

Being widowed, he harbored a strong aversion to ever marrying again. His short marriage had been a disaster—as much his fault as his wife's. She had been a silly girl who moved from vapors to elation within minutes. To remove himself from daily hysterics, he had busily pursued all the allure of the pleasures afforded the aristocracy. The two heedless personalities made a failure of marriage.

He had been too young when he married. Since it had been a marriage of convenience, he often wondered why he had agreed to it. He regretted the marriage but not Julie, the blessing of that union. He deplored the fact his little girl had no mother, but he would never marry again.

The Earl of Wentworth was known among his tenants as a fair man and allowed no injustice to fall upon his people by those who represented him on his estates. He was not political in nature, seldom attended to his parliamentary duties, and when he did he rarely spoke.

He now sat in the private parlor of the Royal Rose. He was en route to London to speak in favor of a motion in the House of Lords to honor Lord Viscount Wellington for the victory under his command at Talavera. After all, Wellington was a fellow countryman and friend; he could do no less.

His lordship gratefully stretched out his long legs and sipped a glass of ale. The coach had been confining, but he had remained inside to occupy Julie on the long journey. Two more days and they would make London. Not a moment too soon, he thought.

It was difficult for active little ones to remain confined in a coach, so he had played games with his daughter until he was exhausted. Odd how children never seem to tire. A smile played briefly on his lips at the thought of her gleeful laughter when she won. He had arranged she did so frequently, just to hear her squeals of delight.

Nanny Rourke had smiled on their play with approval, but now and again she had clucked her tongue against her teeth at his indulgence. Often at odds with him on that very subject, she made it her mission to see that the motherless child did not become too spoiled. She genuinely cared for Julie and tempered love with good, solid training. Nanny made her practical views known.

His lordship would shrug his broad shoulders at her suggestions. His daughter would have the best, and no more tragedy would enter her life if he could prevent it. A sliver of guilt hovered in the back of his mind. Would Mary, his wife, have fought harder to live had they been happy? Was it his failings that ultimately led his daughter to be motherless?

He refused to entertain the thought any longer and rose from the chair to find out what in the devil was keeping the innkeeper with his dinner. He was famished. Nanny Rourke had taken Julie to their bedroom straightaway. He ordered a meal immediately upon their arrival, for Nanny and Julie were tired and hungry, too.

Before Sir Julian reached the door, it burst open and Simmons, his valet, rushed in, followed by the breathless, red-faced innkeeper.

"Your lordship, something terrible has happened! It is outrageous, unthinkable!" Simmons said in a voice indicating more affront than he had ever previously displayed during his long employment.

Fear struck at his lordship's heart. He paled. "Julie?"

"Oh, no, no. Nothing like that. But some widow has commandeered your room," Simmons said, waiting for the outrage to register on his lordship's face. He was disappointed. Only a blank look of incomprehension appeared.

"Someone has taken my room?"

"Your lordship, let me explain," the innkeeper chimed in, all the while wringing his hands. "She has two huge ruffians who barged in and removed your luggage and had it placed in the one I had provided in exchange."

No such affront had ever happened to his lordship before, and he stood in disbelief. He was momentarily speechless. "Well, we shall see to that." He began to spring into action just as a slender lady in widow weeds appeared at the doorway, flanked by two giants just spoiling for a fight.

"Allow me to explain," the widow said. Her voice was soft and lilting and carried a heavy accent of the north country. He could not see her face—the veil was too heavy—but her figure indicated she was young. She stepped forward. Her gorilla-sized escorts stepped forward, flanking her in a menacing challenge.

His lordship gave a perfunctory bow. "Please do. I am curious as to what precipitated this vulgar scene."

Claire's cheeks flushed and her eyes flashed and stung with tears of anger at his despicable rebuke. Thank heavens for her veil! She stood resolute, trying to hold her ground.

All eyes looked toward her, and she realized it was indeed an ignoble scene. She was momentarily mute and felt witless, her mind scampering for a setdown.

Aware of Claire's discomfort, Phoebe stepped past Will and gently took her niece's arm. The diminutive lady pulled herself up to her full sixty inches and met the nobleman's eyes without quailing.

"My lord, my niece had written weeks ago to secure this private room and the best bedchamber. As you can see, we are in need of privacy, with the sorrow of our recent bereavement. It seems you have usurped us and bagged them for your use. Since we are now forced to eat in our bedchamber, we have taken the room that provides the space to do so. It is far more vulgar for you to prey upon a defenseless widow and then insult her," Phoebe said, continuing to meet his eyes.

"Hardly defenseless," the earl muttered as he sent an appraising glance to their husky retinue. He felt the urge to knock the smug grins off their faces. He was a master at fisticuffs and could have easily done so. He looked to the innkeeper. "Is this true?"

"Well, your lordship, I . . . that is . . ."

Aunt Phoebe offered a superior smile and a slight curtsy and turned to lead the way out of the private parlor. Claire, angry, then Will and Jamie, triumphant, followed her into the hall.

"We'll finish our dinner, then take turns guarding your door," Will said as he and Jamie headed once more toward the taproom. "Call us if you need us again."

"That will not be necessary. I would not dream of inconveniencing the *widow* again. My pardons, madam." The earl's voice was low and resonant. He stood at the door of the private dining room leaning insolently against the jamb, arms crossed over his broad chest and a mocking glint to his vivid jade eyes.

At the sound of his voice, Claire turned and said, "See that you do not." Continuing up the steps, she thought he had chuckled, but she could not be sure. If it was his laughter, then that only went to prove he was no gentleman in his obvious condescension.

"Claire!" Phoebe snapped when they had made the sanctuary of the bedchamber. "How could you get us into such a vulgar, vulgar scene?"

"I hate him!"

"Who?"

"That arrogant duke or whatever he is."

"*Hate* him? You don't even know him. We agreed to keep an inconspicuous existence until we completed all the appropriate background for you. The first moment out of the gate and you have us in a brawl in the hall of a common inn. Child, whatever is the matter with you? Has a little money suddenly gone to your head?"

"That's not it and you know it," Claire said defensively.

"All I know is that you did not behave like the lady you are going to pretend to be. You will mend your ways before we set a single foot in London, or you will pass for no more than a parlor maid!"

"He made me angry! He looked so very satisfied with himself," Claire said, removing her bonnet and veil.

"Frankly, I thought him uncommonly attractive.

I am glad you had the veil down. If we should meet him again, perhaps he will not recognize you."

"I hope I never meet him again!"

"Why are you taking on so? Most noblemen are arrogant. You are the one who wants to join their ranks. Great Scott, child, you behaved like a fishwife. I could not believe my ears or eyes. One does not confront a total stranger. We could have made do with the smaller bedroom."

"You are the one who told him he preyed on defenseless widows."

Claire looked white and drawn. Phoebe's scold came to an abrupt halt.

"I had to step in. He obviously left you speechless. Now, dear, let us forget the incident and order some dinner and get a good night's rest. You are merely irritable from the long, tiring trip."

Claire sent her a chastened glance. "I behaved badly, I admit. But it just sent me into a high dudgeon to think he could waltz in and take our rooms just because he is some aristocrat."

"You will have to learn to ignore rudeness. In all probability, he was never told the rooms had been previously engaged. The innkeeper is certainly more likely to wish to please a duke or earl or whatever he is than two country ladies in mourning."

"Country? How would they know?"

"They have ears, don't they?"

"Than I shall add elocution lessons to my list when we reach Bath."

"Good. Until then, I suggest you keep your mouth closed."

Claire laughed. Phoebe joined in, but her laugh carried a hint of nervousness. This widow business and sudden wealth were making her more anxious by the moment.

Her niece had been kept in harness far too long, and it was going to take more than vigilance to keep her out of scrapes.

"Claire, you must act very circumspect if anyone is going to believe you are a widow. If you cannot manage it, I suggest you drop the charade and carry on as you truly are."

"I promise I shall not repeat such a foolish action. I realize now it was incredibly stupid to call attention to myself that way. Perhaps it was a good thing it happened. You see, I learned my lesson."

"Hmm, perhaps."

"Still, I do hate men like him. So high and mighty. He called me base, common! If ever I have the chance, I shall get even with him!"

"Claire, there you go again! You just this moment vowed you'd behave in a very proper manner. Next you're vowing revenge. Child, come to your senses, or it is back to Rosehill."

Claire laughed. "Oh, Phoebe, let me spread my wings a bit. I shall be a pattern card of sober behavior. I promise."

"Yes, dear. It is definitely to your advantage that you do. You want to dance at some famous balls and be escorted to the opera and all those delights of society. You will get there only by minding your p's and q's. I have spent some time in society, and you can ruin your reputation beyond repair with

58

the least infraction. The first lesson is that a lady does not draw attention to herself!"

Claire nodded and primly folded her hands. "Like this?"

"Exactly," Phoebe said, then answered the knock on the door. Servants brought in a cart with covered dishes. Dinner was being served at last. Phoebe could not wait to eat and retire. The day had been too long and beyond her liking. She glanced at Claire, who sat demurely quiet as the dishes were set out. Perhaps all would work out satisfactorily. . . . But she was not convinced by her optimistic thought.

Seven

"While they ready the coach and strap on the luggage, I want to walk in the small garden at the back of the inn. Do you wish to come?" Claire asked Phoebe, who was pouring a second cup of chocolate.

"No, dear, I want to finish this, and I will join you in a few minutes. I do not think it will be long before we are on our way."

Claire tied her bonnet ribbons and took up her black gloves. "I shall meet you in the courtyard. I am so restless, and I do not know why. Perhaps a little walk will stretch my legs and calm me. Tell Will or Jamie to fetch me when all is ready."

The inviting garden was small and well tended. A greater portion was devoted to vegetables for the inn's kitchen. The early peas and lettuce were cleverly placed behind the primroses. She wondered at and admired the mind behind this arrangement. The idea of adding beauty to the necessary was clever indeed. No doubt it was the overworked wife of the innkeeper.

When life became settled, she would spend time

in creating a garden of great beauty. Now she had the means to hire the needed gardeners.

She realized, quite to her surprise, that a garden was high on her list of wishes. It occurred to her that it surpassed her wish to cut a dash. Perhaps London society was not her true desire. No matter—she would taste it all before she donned a lace cap. If she did not care for the stimulating life of London, she would simply leave.

After the matters of business were settled in London, she and Phoebe would go directly to Bath. Her decision to live there during her "mourning period" was the correct one.

Many retired members of the ton who had social position resided among those seeking the beneficial waters, and they needed connections before attempting to enter London society. It was probably the only way they would manage to do so. She knew absolutely no one in London.

The spring sun was warm and welcoming, and she felt a surge of elation. Her vague disquiet faded. The excitement of new experiences lured her with the greatest expectations. That surely explained her restive feelings.

When she tired of society, she told herself, they would simply retire to wherever they wished. Perhaps, when the terrible war ended, they would travel the continent. Aunt Phoebe would dote on that. She smiled with satisfaction at the threshold of her new life. No need to worry, she told herself. Her fears were foolish.

Coming across a stone bench along the walk, she

sat to admire the flowers and absorb the solitude. Lifting her veil, she closed her eyes, turned her face to the warm sun, and sighed with contentment.

"Hello, my name is Julie. What's yours?"

The small voice broke her reverie, and Claire looked down in surprise to find an engaging little girl standing before her. The child was expensively dressed, a bit too lavishly for one so young. Her large, candid blue eyes and the mass of dark curls peeking out of her bonnet made an enchanting picture. The child smiled up at Claire with no hint of shyness.

Claire returned her smile but quickly glanced around to find an adult. The child was far too young to be left alone.

"Where is your mother?"

"I don't have one; she's gone to heaven."

At first Claire did not know how to respond. The child obviously had strayed off. Surely whoever was in charge should have more sense than to allow a child this young out of his sight.

"My mother has gone to heaven, too. Come sit beside me, and tell me who should be watching you."

"Are you sad?" Julie asked.

"Sad?"

" 'Cause your mother's gone to heaven."

"She has been gone a long time. I miss her, but I am not sad. Are you?"

"I don't remember my mother. Nanny Rourke takes care of me. My papa is taking us to London. He has promised to show me a place where there are wild animals. Are you going to London to see the animals?"

"Yes, I am going to London, but only for a few days, so I doubt I shall have time to visit the wild animals. I think we should find your Nanny Rourke before she becomes worried. We would not want her to feel lost, now, would we?" Claire put her arm around the child and gave her a small hug. The child returned the smile and snuggled into Claire's arm.

"You are pretty," Julie said.

"Julie! I have been frantic to find you." The low, masculine voice caused them to start and turn in the direction from which it had come.

Claire was surprised she had not heard his approach, but there he stood, tall and looming. The blazing sun was behind him, and his shadow fell across her lap. The towering man was handsome— far more so than she had remembered. His expression was as disagreeable as it had been the previous night.

"Papa, I met a new friend. She is going to London. Mayhap she can come to have tea with me."

Claire looked unflinchingly into the eyes of the antagonistic man who had displaced them the previous evening. She pursed her lips in disapproval and rose, still holding Julie's hand.

"It is quite dangerous for her to be unattended. I should think you would take more care. There are horses in the courtyard; she could easily be hurt." Her words carried a sharp, scolding tone and clear disdain.

A flicker of anger crossed his cold, jade-colored eyes, and a muscle moved in his jaw. He did not take reprimands lightly. In fact, he was never addressed in such a manner. Besides, he felt a sting of guilt, for the shrew was right, and he did not appreciate her pointing it out to him.

"The Earl of Wentworth, at your service," he said, and offered an exaggerated bow. "I am astonished at your interest. You had not struck me as one whose concern lay in such directions. Come, Julie, we must leave; Nanny is worried. Thank the woman for watching out for you."

Claire's cheeks flamed red and her hands closed into tiny, hard fists. The desire to strike him washed over her. *Woman!* How dare he! He pointedly had not called her a lady! That was the second time he had indicated she was lowborn! The cur!

Lord Wentworth held his eyes steady and took in every detail of her fetching face. She may be a shrew, but, by God, no one could deny her beauty. Odd, he thought, how frequently the beauties are the most disagreeable. He presumed they learned to depend on their appearance and failed to develop a pleasant demeanor.

"Come, Julie." He reached out and took his daughter's hand, then turned to leave.

"I suggest, Earl Whatever, that you take heed of your responsibilities henceforth," Claire called after him.

He paused but did not turn around. The stinging truth of her remark infuriated him. Her husband had probably died to get away from her bad temper. The thought did not mollify his ire.

Claire stood motionless as they left. Little Julie turned and waved, and Claire returned the motion. People should not have children if they cannot be bothered to watch them, she thought. The arrogance of the man! He was rude beyond measure. Was this the nature of the aristocratic society she was planning to join? The brightness of her adventure began to fade. Well, one rude man should not condemn them all.

She turned her steps toward the courtyard. The coach must be ready by now. The sooner they got away, the better it would be. She hoped she would never meet him again.

Her mind was going over every detail of her encounter with the disagreeable earl, thinking of perfect setdowns she wished she had thought of at the time. Deep in her thoughts, she entered the courtyard, failing to notice the mounted horseman galloping across the cobblestones. She stepped directly into his path.

Her mind reeled in fright as the sounds of terror closed on her ears. She raised her hands in a feeble attempt to ward off the onslaught of hooves.

A strong arm clamped around her body, knocking the air out of her lungs. She was swung up and around so fast, she did not know what was happening. The horse missed her by inches as the rider sped on and out of the yard.

Claire struggled for air, and her legs buckled under her. Her bonnet fell back as she leaned into the strong arms that held her in a viselike grip. She gasped, and the world dimmed.

It was only seconds, which seemed like years, before she stopped trembling and strength began to return to her legs. She was safe, but she still leaned into the arms that held her.

When her heart began to slow its runaway pace, she placed weight on her wobbly legs. She rested a moment in the powerful arms and tried to gather her scattered wits.

"I suggest you use a little common sense and take care when entering a busy inn courtyard. You could have been maimed or killed." The earl's low, resonant voice stabbed through her brain.

Recognition of the voice from the lips so close to her ear dawned on her fuzzy brain. Her eyes flew open, and she looked directly into the face of the scowling earl. His eyes pierced hers, then flickered with an unrecognizable emotion. His mouth was only inches away. His grip tightened.

Incapable of resisting, she remained a second gathering her strength and thoughts. Their eyes held in mutual dislike, yet something intimate, sensual, and primordial passed between them, a shocking awareness that lit a fire not soon to be extinguished.

"Are you quite recovered?" he asked, gently placing her on her own two feet. The sensation of her soft, feminine body pressed against his sent a flash of sexual desire, totally unexpected and decidedly unwelcome. He struggled to regain his self-contained demeanor.

"Yes. How reckless of me. I wasn't thinking. It happened so fast." Her words were whispered in weak disbelief.

"Then perhaps you can understand an omission happening to others." The rancor in his voice was clear, and Claire blushed with chagrin.

His eyes flickered over her again. He bent to pick up Julie, who had begun to cry. Carrying the frightened child, he crossed the courtyard, leaving Claire standing at the edge, still pale and trembling. He knew he should escort her into the inn, but his only thought was to get away—fast.

Adjusting her bonnet with trembling fingers, Claire hurried to her waiting coach just as Phoebe and the Dalton brothers emerged from the inn. They were ready to leave and apparently had not seen the foolish incident.

She felt incredibly stupid at her carelessness, and she offered herself the excuse that Rosehill certainly provided no lessons on looking out for traffic. It was a lesson well learned, for surely London must teem with vehicles and horses. She just wished it had not been the earl to the rescue.

The earl's crested traveling coach pulled abreast of theirs just as Claire entered hers and took the seat next to the window. She was only a few feet away from the earl, Julie, and her nursemaid. The maid looked chastened, and Claire didn't doubt for a minute that the woman had felt the sting of his aristocratic tongue.

"Good-bye," Julie called to Claire as she was lifted up inside the vehicle.

"Good-bye. Enjoy London and the animals," Claire called back.

The earl turned and looked at her. He stepped forward. "What is your name? I do not believe you mentioned it."

"I did not."

"Surely you do not deny me the name of the lady I so gallantly saved?" He smiled, showing even teeth and a devilish twinkle in his eyes.

"I do thank you, but you have no need of my name," Claire said just as the coachman cracked his whip, sending their horses into motion.

"I am the Earl of Wentworth," he called to the departing coach. "Wentworth," he muttered softly. "You may have need of it someday."

Eight

"Jamie, why are we stopping here?" Claire called out the carriage window. Her surprise reverberated in the pitch of her voice. The coach came to a halt in the courtyard of the Black Falcon Inn, which stood on the road leading into London.

Hearing his mistress's plaintive call, Jamie swung down from his horse and hurried to the side of the coach. "It's the horses," he answered. "They are done in. Ain't gonna go much farther. This old coach is mighty heavy, and we have gone as far as we can today."

Fields, the coachman, jumped down from the box and headed toward them, nodding in agreement. His ruddy face glowed with excitement as he spoke. "Aye, mistress, he's right. We can't go on with them. We will have to spend the night to rest them." He shook his head and shrugged his shoulders. "We knew they were not prime animals when we bought 'em. Still, they've done better than ever I thought."

"But we are so near London! Surely we can hire

fresh horses!" Claire said, climbing down from the vehicle as soon as Fields let down the steps.

Moving more slowly in answer to stiff, aching joints, Phoebe scrambled out as best she could. Claire was annoyed they had stopped, but she was grateful. A wee stretch of her legs was welcome.

"It makes no difference whether we make London tonight or not. We could rest here, then go on. . . ." Phoebe said. Her voice faded with her conviction as she viewed the shabby inn.

Reading Phoebe's mind, Fields said, "I'll look into horses for hire. If possible, we'd best continue. Ain't a likely place for the two of you, I'm thinking. I'll go around to the stables and see if horses are available to us."

Claire shook out her skirts, dropped her veil, and accompanied Phoebe toward the inn. The taproom was almost empty. She glanced around the room and saw only a few patrons.

"May we have a private parlor where we can wait? Are there fresh horses for hire?" Claire asked the proprietor when he bustled up to greet them.

"Unfortunately, we are but a small inn, as you can see," he said, sweeping his hand for her agreement. "We have no private parlors, but come, sit here. You will not be bothered, I assure you. Can I bring you some tea? We have fresh scones, too."

"It will do, Claire. Yes, my good man, some tea, indeed. I am in sore need of some," Phoebe chirped up, and followed him to a table in a corner.

Claire trailed behind in forbearance; there was little else she could do. As they crossed the room to be seated, she noticed a wounded soldier sitting across the room, and she felt a pang as her heart went out to him. He had been grievously injured, for he wore an eye patch and his left arm in a sling. A cane leaned against the table, adding to the mood of melancholy that surrounded him, as did his pale skin tightly drawn over his handsome features. He sat motionless, staring out the window.

Claire thought it odd that his air of sad resignation seemed to reach across the room and touch her so personally. It was beyond sympathy; it was as if she knew him.

Seated across from the officer was a young lady who spoke in whispered words. She was talking, but it seemed he was not listening. The young lady eventually fell silent.

Claire's interest was drawn to the couple many times. There was something that captured her attention besides the obvious fact that he was a hero of the terrible war with France. I'm staring, she thought, and took up the welcome tea that had been placed before them.

Quietly sipping the hot tea and nibbling fresh scones, Claire found it impossible to hide her vexation. The trip was near its end, and she was utterly annoyed that they could not complete it now.

She hated this delay, and she would hate it more if they had to spend the night. In a few hours they could be in London! Exhilarating, bustling London!

Claire's thoughts were interrupted when another soldier entered the taproom with her coachman, Fields, at his side and the Dalton boys trailing behind. Passing by, they crossed the room and fell into an animated conversation with the wounded military officer. On one occasion the officer glanced toward them, then turned back to the coachman. He nodded and started to rise. His young female companion motioned for him to remain seated and spoke to Claire's coachman, who then proceeded to cross the room toward their table.

"Miss Darington, a stroke of fortune for us. Major Tyndall, his sister, and his aide are also en route to London. They find themselves stranded with a carriage problem that cannot be fixed in short order. However, they have a fresh team of outstanding grays," Fields said, indicating with his hand that the seated major was the one of whom he spoke. The major's aide was headed in her direction.

"Sergeant Malcombe, at your service," the scarlet-coated gentleman said with a smart bow. "It is our understanding that you are as anxious to reach London as we. Actually, it is imperative that we do so as soon as possible. Since it would suit our purposes to join forces, would you consider allowing Major Tyndall and his sister to accompany you in your coach with our team of horses? I shall, of course, ride outside."

They all began to speak at once. Claire glanced at Phoebe and then toward the seated officer at the window table. Their eyes met a moment, and she saw his plea. She looked again to Phoebe. "What do you think?"

"I think it is a prayer answered. The option of

staying here is hardly tempting. We will be safe enough, since we have the twins as outriders and our coachman will be handling the reins. Yes, it is a godsend. Take the offer. Let us get to London as soon as possible. I am as fatigued as you, or more so."

Claire patted Phoebe's hand. Her aunt was not young, and the journey must be exhausting for her.

"Yes, hitch up their team and we'll join forces to make London before nightfall," Claire said, and glanced once more to the seated couple.

They had been traveling for an hour, and Claire could not resist repeated peeks at the wounded officer. A strained, pale aura surrounded the major and pinched his fine features. He seemed so fragile, as though he were just able to hang on. Claire's concern grew with each mile.

He rested with his eyes closed, listening to the ladies' conversation, or so it seemed, for he would signal agreement when pressed to do so by his sister, Eileen.

Eileen Tyndall was lively and pretty and obviously adored her brother. Her blue eyes snapped with expression, as did the smile that frequented her lips. She turned to Major Tyndall repeatedly for his affirmation of what she had just expounded.

The major would make some small comment or noise, and occasionally his lids fluttered open: He was in pain, Claire was sure, and she longed to silence the prattling girl.

"We do not know what our situation shall be,"

Eileen said confidentially, and with the eagerness of one who had not recently had someone in whom to confide. This was true, for she had spent the past weeks tending her brother.

"Since Nathaniel is to be on half pay until he recovers, we shall have to limit our activities," Miss Tyndall disclosed.

Surprised by the candor of her speech, Claire glanced toward the major, who she was now certain was sleeping blissfully.

"I think we had best whisper, or stop talking for a while—your brother has finally gone to sleep. Let him rest," Claire said, and smiled as Miss Tyndall quite agreed.

"The lamb," Miss Tyndall continued, "he is so brave. He was wounded at Talavera, you know. It is not likely he shall be able to continue his military career. Of course, Nelson did, so perhaps Nate can, too, but I doubt it. I worry so about him. He is unbearable when idle. If only he can find a position in London. He is brilliant with figures and a born organizer. He certainly runs me in prime military fashion." She laughed at her quip, turned to the passing landscape, and fell silent.

The countryside passed in review, and the ladies commented on its beauty. The harmony of mutual need between the ladies grew into the harmony of companions. The equanimity brought an intimacy quite unlike any of so short an acquaintance. It sprang from both parties' need of companionship stemming from a recent period of misfortune. And so the miles passed, and the fellow travelers

rought together by coincidence came together by
eed and now joined in friendship. Their conversa-
ion flowed as that of friends of long standing.

"May I ask for whom you mourn?" Miss Tyndall
eventually asked, unable to resist her curiosity.

"My husband," Claire said.

"Her stepfather," Phoebe answered in unison.

Miss Tyndall's eyes widened, and Major Tyndall
sat up in notice. He had been observing the growing friendship.

"Loss of two dearly loved ones! How frightful! I
am so sorry. I should not have asked. You must be
devastated!" Miss Tyndall was shocked to hear of
such a tragedy. Her admiration of the widow soared.
Never had she seen such bravery. She, at least, still
had Nathaniel.

"Madam, may I extend my condolences and beg
you to forgive the intrusion and poor manners of
my sister," Major Tyndall said, and sent a speaking
glance of reproach to his sister.

Phoebe and Claire looked at each other in horror.
They had not lied well! Claire blushed at her deception. She felt like some impostor, which, of
course, she was.

"Well, actually, it is not quite what it seems. I
shall explain it to you, but please, never reveal it
to anyone.

"I am in mourning for my stepfather, whom I do
not actually mourn. He was a harsh man, and it is
no less than release from having to live under the
same roof," Claire said while absently smoothing

her skirt and blushing again. She still carried guilt for not feeling despondent that Simon was gone.

"I am going to London on business matters. Then Aunt Phoebe and I shall go to Bath during our mourning period. It is our thought that Bath will afford me time to learn the ways of society."

Aunt Phoebe frowned at Claire in caution at revealing their plans. Claire ignored the signal. The Tyndalls sat listening to her words with unabashed interest and expectation that commanded Claire to continue.

The Tyndalls listened to Claire's compelling tale, totally captured by her words, each for a different reason. The freedom to come and go as one should please was envied by Miss Tyndall. The idea of arranging one's life circumstances to suit one's desire was totally riveting to the major. When Claire had finished, his admiration of the idea was immense. He took a moment to examine the comely face of the adventuresome "widow."

"What is your name to be? How are you choosing the dear, departed husband? And may I be so bold as to tread on your sensibilities by asking how he met his demise?" Major Tyndall asked, a twinkle in his eye.

Claire returned his smile and warmed to his humor and his response. "I have not found a name, but he died a sad death—in battle on the Peninsular."

"Ah, there I can be of some assistance. Many of my comrades fell there, and, as you can see, I fared only a little better. I can give you a regiment and battle, for you will need some details to drop in conversation. However, you will not require too many. I am sure it is all too 'painful' for you to speak of in much detail."

"Exactly, sir. You quite understand. I do need some history, for if I just make someone up, I will have no foundation and it will not ring of the truth. I need some obscure officer who had no close family. One whose aunt or cousin I shall not meet at some function."

"I am convinced that the home office is in need of your services. You are a born tactician." Major Tyndall chuckled. "I shall give you your husband shortly, but let me think on it a moment."

Miss Tyndall sat wide-eyed. Imagine actually doing such a thing! "Why do you need to be a widow?"

"I am eight and twenty and firmly on the shelf. As a widow out of mourning, I shall give balls, go to the opera, and do as I please. I am going to buy the most dashing carriage and team of horses. I intend to set London on its ear. I shall cut such a dash that no spinster would be allowed without censure. We have been buried in the country, and now I intend to see the glittering world of the ton. I can afford to do so, and so I shall."

Miss Tyndall clapped her hands. "How famous! I envy you. I should be making my come-out, but now we must postpone it. We must wait until Nate is well and we are properly settled."

Claire felt a twinge in her heart; she knew what it was to wait. The young should not have to postpone life. She smiled at Miss Tyndall in understanding. Life was seldom fair. The young lady must wait because her brother served his country heroically. How unfair.

They continued on in silence while an idea formed in Claire's head. She had been extremely frank with the Tyndalls, and she did not even know them! That fact alone amazed her. Her next move was to amaze her even more, and just about send Aunt Phoebe into a tizzy.

"Major Tyndall, I have an offer to make. You are in need of a position and I am in need of someone to act as secretary to me. I need someone to handle my daily affairs, for instance, to choose a carriage and horses and negotiate a lease on a house. Actually, a million things, a myriad of details about which I know nothing. My man of business could not possibly attend to all that I require. Would you consider taking such a post with me?"

Major Tyndall was so taken aback, he was speechless. The idea of a position was tempting. He had been sick with worry about their future. He stared, unable to answer.

"Of course, we shall take your sister under our wing. We shall give her a come-out, and that will suit my purposes precisely! What better excuse for going to London and setting about to entertain? What better opportunity than the introduction of a young lady into society? Do you have the entry into society?"

"I do indeed. I can do all that you speak of and more. I do not have the funds to present Eileen, but

I have the pedigree. You see, I am the son of the second wife of Baron Tyndall.

"I have even managed a husband for you. He died in my company, leaving no close family members in England. I believe he had an older relative in Ireland who bought him his commission.

"This relative came into some sort of title in Ireland from a distant family line. I cannot remember what the title was, if Richard ever mentioned it. Since my friend never spoke much of his family, I assume they were not close and that he seldom goes to London. It is perfect," Major Tyndall said. The pallor that had hovered about him lifted a little with his enthusiasm.

"I think we must give it a try out in Bath. We shall see how we all get on," Claire said.

"Agreed."

"Major Tyndall, we shall talk about salary and details at a more appropriate time. Now kindly tell me who I am."

"Why, Mrs. Richard Anseley, I knew your husband well. He was the best of men. I am sure it was a terrible shock to lose your husband after so short a marriage. I will tell you, he was a fine soldier— died a hero. There was such honesty in his brown eyes, and his tall bearing was proudly military, don't you agree?"

"Yes, Major Tyndall, Richard was a noble man indeed. I do believe his warm brown eyes were one of the things that first attracted me to him."

"Good, I think we shall manage very well indeed.

When we return from Bath to take up residence in London, you will be errorless."

"Major Tyndall, could you teach me to dance?"

"My wounds will not allow me to dance, but we shall find a dancing master for both you and Eileen, although my sister is quite accomplished. Mayhap I could polish your French?"

"You would have to begin at the beginning; I know no French," Claire said.

"Naturellement je le ferai," he said, and offered a charming smile.

Nine

London

$\mathcal{M}$r. Gibbons stood in the middle of the babbling assemblage in utter amazement at the number of people now connected with Miss Darington's soon-to-be London establishment. They included: Miss Darington, Miss Phoebe Greene, a Major Tyndall, his sister, Miss Tyndall, Mr. Fields, the coachman, and two strapping retainers or footmen or whatever their position was.

The group stood in the middle of the drawing room, staring and talking simultaneously about the merits of the small but charming house he had selected. Gibbons could not imagine why Miss Darington would have all her household in tow during her inspection. He was soon to find out.

"As you can see—" Claire's hand swept the direction of her entourage "—it will not do. The house is charming, but I need more room."

"Ain't even a stable or muse to one," Jamie complained, with Will nodding in disapproving agreement.

"I shall need an office to carry out my duties," Major Tyndall said in a gentle reminder.

"We shall be entertaining when our mourning period is over, so a ballroom is imperative," Claire said, turning from the window that overlooked a perfectly tended garden.

"I should, however, like to have a garden as charming as this one. My apologies, I did not know my requirements would be this large when I commissioned you to find a house."

Mr. Gibbons gave a curt nod, but he was not able to hide his consternation. He was standing in the midst of some kind of democracy, one in which the servants had voice equal to that of the mistress! He'd never encountered such a thing. Great Scott, what was this world coming to? It occurred to him to wonder just who was to attend her balls. She might be wealthy, but she was obviously not of the ton. Ennobling disdain crossed his closed features. "I don't know of another, but ... I shall find a larger establishment."

"Mr. Gibbons, you are much too busy to trouble yourself with so many details on my behalf. Major Tyndall has agreed to take the post of my secretary while he recovers from his war injuries. We shall put it to him to secure the proper house, carriage, and horses. Does that meet with your approval?"

Gibbons sighed in relief as he nervously fingered his watch fob. It had occurred to him that Miss Darington was, among her other foibles, not going to be easy to please.

"I think that is a wise decision. I shall, of course, assist him in any manner I can."

Claire returned the polite smile and added, "There is one other matter of business. I am not Miss Darington; I am Mrs. Anseley, widow. My marriage was a secret kept from my stepfather, and now that he has hopefully gone to his reward, I can freely announce it. When last we met, I had not yet learned of my husband's very sad and noble demise on the battlefield." She flourished a small linen handkerchief and dabbed her eyes.

Gibbons's eyes boggled. He could discern no tears, and an uncanny feeling that all was not conventional crept into his mind. His eyes traveled over the faces of her entourage, meeting sorrowful expressions and nods of somber agreement.

" 'Tis a sad thing, it is," Miss Phoebe Greene said, managing a little sniffle. Claire covered her mouth to hide an emerging smile. Aunt Phoebe could not find employment in Covent Garden, she thought.

"He died in my arms," Major Tyndall explained, with undeniable truth in his voice. "A braver man you could not find."

A silence settled over the assembly as they remained staring at Mr. Gibbons, waiting for his reaction.

"I am shocked and offer my condolences. If I had but known, I assure you, Miss . . . er . . . Madam . . . er . . . Mrs. Anseley that I remain your devoted servant. Call on me whenever you need my assistance. Meanwhile, I shall continue to oversee your invest-

ments," Gibbons said, backing toward the entranc
He could not wait to take his leave of this high
unconventional assembly. Were they all mad, o
was he?

Mr. Gibbons may have been appalled by the a
tive participation of Mrs. Anseley's servants, bu
he would have been even more impressed by th
accomplishments of the team workers achieved i
a week's time. The widow Anseley's retinue ma
have been unconventional, but it was efficient.

A residence that was to be available after Janu
ary was found in Portman Square. The house, o
perfect proportions, faced the square, as did all th
houses, with streets between to accommodate car
riages. The square was surrounded by an iron rai
ing to protect the lovely garden. Each resident wa
provided a key so that they might all enjoy th
pleasant parkland, with its fountains and carefull
tended beds. The footpath wound its way among th
gardens and trees. It was an oasis in the bustlin,
heart of London for the resident families of Por
man Square. Claire was delighted by these sur
roundings and looked gratefully to Major Tyndal
for such foresight.

Nathaniel Tyndall smiled into her upturned, an
imated face as she effusively thanked him. The re
ward of seeing her happiness was all the impetu
he needed to spur him on to greater heights o
pleasing her. His gaze lingered on her sparklin
eyes, his heart constricting.

Claire could think of no improvements, but Tyn

dall made a few suggestions to add to her future comfort in the house. By now Claire was amazed not only at his eye for detail but also his ability to get things done.

"It was a lucky day for me when my horses gave out and your coach axle broke," she said quietly.

He laughed. "Indeed, indeed. Eileen and I are ever grateful for that stroke of luck or providential blessing. But now, madam, you must come take a peek at the carriage and horses."

Claire squealed with delight when she emerged from the entrance of the hotel. There stood a landau with a pair of beautifully matched grays. It sported varnished panels with decorative paint work and thin green-and-yellow striping.

"The green leather is perfect, and look at all the brass trim!" Claire exclaimed, and turned to a beaming Major Tyndall. "The choice is perfect. It exceeds my expectations! I could not have done better. Think how dashing I shall be."

They remained at the Hotel Claredon, which was noted for its respectability and was certainly well suited for a widow, her family, and her servants.

Major Tyndall continued proving to be the epitome of efficiency. He took each task in hand and issued the orders to bring them into being with the dispatch of Wellington. His health was still very precarious, but Will and Jamie became his legs, and they responded to every task with the strength and verve of youth.

Claire was glad to keep the boys too occupied to

get into trouble. Mischief was readily available in London, and she had promised their mama that she would see they kept out of the dens of iniquity. Major Tyndall also kept a keen eye on the lads, and she was grateful for his watchful concern. She was sure he would know what to look for and thereby head off mischief.

Claire realized she was becoming more dependent on Major Tyndall with each passing day.

Since they were to be in London for so short a time, the ladies spent two entire days with the mantuamaker and employed a host of seamstresses in uncounted hours of fitting and sewing. Claire and Phoebe were provided with elegant wardrobes of mourning and half mourning. Eileen was provided the modest dresses of a young lady yet to make her come-out.

Claire marveled at her previous naïveté in thinking that she could have managed all this on her own. Nathaniel Tyndall was truly the godsend she had unknowingly needed. She grew more grateful for his help as each task was completed.

Ten

Claire entered Hatchard's on Piccadilly the afernoon before their departure and began to browse he library stacks. Her entourage trailed behind ike ducks behind their mother and so far exceeded ociety's dictates on being properly chaperoned as o be excessive. Claire had vowed to be the most correct widow in all Christendom and thereby be known as a stickler for propriety.

She was accompanied by Aunt Phoebe and her new abigail, Dora, who immediately took a seat with Will on a bench outside the shop. Claire had noted Dora's mooning gaze cast in Will's direction on more than one occasion. She could hardly fault the girl; the Dalton lads were manly young men. Will, however, seemed to take no note of the slip of a girl.

Claire was occupied with their transfer to Bath, which she hoped would be the beginning of her adventure. She clearly understood that she was an unknown and lacked family connections. Aunt Phoebe assured her that Bath was a curious blend of people and held a greater chance for her mingling with those of a higher order. Perhaps not of the first circles, but surely some members of genteel society would befriend her.

Trying to concentrate on the books at hand, she thought there must be something there to amuse her. Hatchard's was hardly a store for mere light hearted reading, for it was considered the most literate bookstore in London.

John Hatchard was a pious bookseller and published, among other things, *The Christian Observer*. The fashionable premises were clublike in creating an atmosphere of subdued intellectual gentility.

Tyndall had sent her here for that purpose alone. For Claire any diversion would do. They had done nothing but work since coming to London. This was hardly her dream of fun and freedom. But at last all was ready. Tomorrow they would leave for Bath, and she intended to improve her limited knowledge by reading. She turned the pages of one of the latest novels of no social redeeming value—hardly the stuff with which to edify oneself.

"Good afternoon." The low, resonant voice broke into her deliberation. Without thinking, she responded by turning to its source. Instantly regretting it, she stared into the face of the nobleman who had unceremoniously taken her reserved rooms on her journey to London. His jade eyes held hers for a split second.

A tumultuous tumble in her chest brought a blushing response at her quick reaction to him. She was able, nevertheless, to summon a blank exression. Hastily turning to look behind her (as if ssuming he must be addressing someone else), she hrugged. Certainly he could not be addressing her! he hoped her acting skills were clever enough to arry off that ploy. She ignored him by returning ɔ the perusal of the book she held.

The gentleman was neither fooled nor discour-ged by her conduct. "The Earl of Wentworth, at our service. I trust your continued journey was un-narred." His voice was low, soft and seductive and arried a hint of amusement.

She turned slowly, deliberately, to face him and ;ave him a cold, blank stare. "Sir, you mistake me. do not know you. Please leave."

His eyes trailed leisurely over her upturned face. Ier color was "giveaway heightened," and she was nore beguiling than his dreams of her recalled. Her hick lashes set off her wonderful brown eyes, which eflected flecks of gold that seemed to sparkle with musement. Tiny scattered freckles danced across ier nose and were utterly captivating. He won-lered why most ladies would as soon die before pre-senting their freckles, usually perceived as fflictions, to polite society. They were adorable on ner. He had the strongest urge to kiss each one. She would no doubt set a new fashion for freckles.

Her full mouth was soft and inviting. His eyes lingered on it, resulting in the almost undeniable urge to kiss that, too. His gaze then traveled again to her eyes, where he detected a flicker. While he could not read its meaning, he had caused some re-action, and he was delighted with any response.

Her arctic glare returned, and she turned and walked away.

He stood helpless, watching her leave. He could hardly chase after her. Damnation! He noted how gracefully she moved and the exquisite cut and quality of her dress. The difference in her attire from their first encounter was marked. Had her circumstances changed or had she just chosen to travel in old, unstylish apparel? In mourning she might be, but she remained totally fascinating.

Clenching his fists, he decided he must find out who she was and somehow get an introduction. He would make inquiries. There must be someone who was a mutual acquaintance. Then he could call on her to extend his apology for any inconvenience he might have caused her. Perhaps he should wait until she was out of mourning. How could he find out when that would be unless he knew who she was?

Suddenly he was appalled at his eagerness, his impetuosity in plotting to seek her out. There had been no one in recent years who had so captured his imagination and interest. He was not pleased with the feeling of necessity she imparted to him. He took pride in keeping his liaisons on an independent footing, at least on his part. He did not mind an adoring female, as long as he remained emotionally uninvolved.

His heart disregarded his mind. He would get on it today. Someone must know who she is, he thought. For one split second he toyed with the idea of following her to find out where she lived. No, that would be totally obnoxious! My God, he told

imself, take control; you are acting like an un-
icked cub. He had time; their paths would cross
gain because he would see to it.

He smiled to himself as he watched her grace-
ully climb into the waiting carriage, assisted by
hat Neanderthal servant of hers. The same elderly
ady accompanied her, as well as her maid. He stood
t the shop window until the carriage was out of
ight.

"May I be of assistance?" the shop clerk asked,
reaking into Wentworth's thoughts. The mer-
hant was taken aback by the ferocious glare the
entleman turned on him and hastily retreated.

Wentworth was still frowning when he stepped
ut into the sunlight. His gaze drifted again in the
lirection of her departure. Get a hold of yourself,
ie admonished.

Perhaps he would pick up a bauble and spend the
fternoon with Belle. She had a way of soothing
iim with her quiet ways. He placed his hat on his
iead and walked to his waiting carriage. He knew he
vould not call on Belle; that affair was now over.
The mystery lady had lit a fire that only she could
extinguish. It had been too long since he had felt
,his way, and he was both pleased and annoyed.

Major Tyndall steadied himself. The room
whirled. He clung to the top of the chest of drawers
and allowed the vertigo to pass. In moments his
breathing became normal, and he straightened his
back. Taking a deep breath, he waited a moment
longer. It was gone.

He looked into the mirror, and his pale face stared back. This was not encouraging. Yet he thought he was getting better with every passing day. He prayed it was so.

Minton, his new valet, busied about in great alarm, still keeping an eye on his master. Displaying no expression, he began arranging the folds of the major's neck cloth. He was well aware he had not won over the major's confidence.

Tyndall was not yet able to dress himself, and he hated every task Minton performed for him. While his arm was definitely better, the dependent feeling was a source of more pain to him than all his injuries added together. He was a proud and independent man. He must bear it and he would, but he did not have to like it.

Tyndall knew the journey to Bath was going to be difficult. It would take all his resources, but it would keep his mind off his pain. How much he could hide was always a question. He hated Eileen's anxious eyes and Claire's anxiety following him whenever he came into their sight. He understood their concern and he could not fault it, no matter how disconcerting it was.

Minton stepped back and declared, "Major, you're in prime fashion now. Although nothing can match a uniform for dash, you look quite the thing. The neck cloth is tied to perfection, if I am allowed the boldness of saying so myself."

Tyndall smiled, took a final look at himself, and decided he would do. While not in the pink of healthy looks, he was not yet about to expire. He smiled to himself and left his room.

Slowly he made his way to the waiting carriage. The call about to be made on Lady Compton was with two motives, both significant. One was to inform Lady Compton of her son's last brave hours, and the other was to mention the Widow Anseley. Both tasks weighed heavily on him.

Jamie waited for him beside the carriage, hovering and trying to appear as though he was not. Tyndall appreciated his interest and had to accept it with charity, for he had no choice. It was tolerable only because he improved daily.

Jamie helped Tyndall into the carriage, then climbed in and took the reins. He set their direction toward Grosvenor Square.

It was a glorious day. Tyndall was gladdened. It was pleasing to be out-of-doors. Amazing how adversity could bring one's attention to the small joys normally taken for granted. A pity, he thought, mankind is prone to take the most important gifts of existence with little regard and dwell on what will pass as of no import.

He could hardly fault the young for their feelings of invulnerability, for he had gone into battle with just such a sense of invincibility! He shook his head. A mistake, he thought, to refine too much on the past. He would enjoy the lovely morning, lest he be equally ungrateful for what providence offered.

They left Albemarle Street and headed through London to Grosvenor Square. The square was one of the largest and most beautiful in all of London.

It claimed aristocrats of the highest order and seemed destined to remain so, with its proximity to Hyde Park.

A very proper butler in red livery and a black arm band ushered him into the house. The interior was darkened by draperies closed against the sun light. The funereal atmosphere clung to the rooms and assailed his heart with a heaviness he realized he had not felt since coming into Mrs. Anseley's employ.

Like so many others, he had promised Compton (before that brave soldier closed his eyes for the last time) he would call upon his mother and sister.

He was glad to oblige a fallen comrade, for he had been truly fond of the young man, but today was perhaps the wrong choice. Sadness still clung to him, and this interview would be difficult. Knowing those left behind held fast to any last words, he was only too happy to bring whatever comfort he could to this grieving family. It was his duty to do so.

When Lady Compton entered, Major Tyndall stiffly and shakily rose to his feet by pushing on his cane.

"Please do not rise for me," Lady Compton said. "Be seated; we do not stand on ceremony. I am more than grateful for your call. I can see you have done so at a price to yourself," she said, crossing the room in a trail of black crepe and a face marked with grief. "Please do sit." She took the settee across from him. "May I send for tea, or perhaps a spot of sherry would warm you?"

"Tea will do nicely, thank you," Tyndall answered, just as the door opened and a slender young lady entered. She was comely even though her eyes bespoke her sorrow. She must be the sister, Tyndall thought. His speculation was proven correct by the introductions that followed.

Her name was Jane Compton, but he had already learned that from her brother's proud conversation when letters arrived from home.

Tea was brought in and silently placed on the table. The servants moved with muted sound and left as quietly. Tyndall's breathing became difficult. The weight of the sorrow was too much for them and beginning to engulf him. He was not strong enough to carry another's pain.

Tyndall stiffened his back and began to tell them of the battle and the circumstances of their loved one's death. They listened with grateful attention, for any word was a small touchstone to him. Quiet questions were asked and Tyndall answered with honesty, deleting the worst details but not holding back any of the true happenings of that costly victory.

The ladies appreciated his honesty and openness sincerely, for they read it in his voice and eyes. Lady Compton was impressed by this handsome young major and admired his grit, for she knew that he was in pain and the memories were difficult.

When at last he finished, Lady Compton thanked him. "You have been most kind to bring us this information. It will help as the days roll on. I am ever grateful, for I know it was not easy. Be assured, you have done me a great service."

They sat in silence, with only the tick of the or molu clock on the mantel. Major Tyndall rose to leave.

"Where can we reach you? I should like to further this acquaintance; that is, if it is agreeable," Lady Compton said, moving to accompany him to the door. A singular honor indeed.

"I have been placed on half pay for a year in hopes my recovery will be sufficient for my return to duty. I am optimistic that will be so."

Lady Jane Compton's voice caught, and her hand raised to her lips in horror of such an idea. Nathaniel turned at her obvious distress and was touched by her concern. She struck him as a singularly charming and delicate young lady.

"Never fear, I shall not likely ever go into battle again. But I could do much needed work elsewhere. For now I have taken a post with Mrs. Anseley."

He then added words that seemed wrong in this situation, and yet he felt his obligation to Claire and his sister.

"She is a recent widow from the ranks of our regiment. Believe me, I am grateful for the post. More importantly she has taken my sister, Eileen, under her wing. Mrs. Anseley has offered to present her when it is appropriate to do so.

"I think the prospect of bringing my sister out next year is offering some diversion to Mrs. Anseley's grief. Since I know little enough about a Season in London, I am most grateful to Mrs. Anseley. They are off to Bath but expect to be back in London next year. I should like to introduce you to her. You have much in common."

"Please do so. Although I do not know her, I should be honored to receive her. But *you* must promise to call again, for I should like to talk more," Lady Compton said, with no effort to hide her pleading tone. Her daughter, Jane, nodded, her eyes on the brink of tears.

"I must take my leave, ladies. I am fatigued."

"But of course, we kept you too long. Please do come again and bring your sister and Mrs. Anseley."

Eleven

𝔅ath was like a staid old dowager, giving way to a younger and more fashionable Brighton, where the beau monde ton flocked behind Prinny to that glittering resort on the English Channel. Bath may have had to bow to Brighton as the favored of the stylish, but she still held the charm of an aging beauty.

The beautiful rolling hills of Somerset slope to the Avon River and the valley where Bath is situated among seven hills, like Rome. Bath's origin is Roman or, at least, as her purpose was set by those interloping conquerors, but her heart is Georgian. Her quaint, comfortable air still drew many visitors, as well as those who came to stay.

In fact, Bath was now attracting older members of society who took it upon themselves to retire where the healing waters might prove advantageous to arthritic aches. Younger members also joined the ranks at Bath for various reasons, such as riding out a storm of scandal, restoring depleted pockets, or healing a broken heart. The residents centered around a desire for a more subdued way of life.

While Bath society had its high sticklers, other members generally lent a more tolerant view on life, which stems from one of the great blessings of growing older. By virtue of having lived long enough to know the foibles of human nature, the older can often shut their eyes and countenance what narrow-minded middle-aged cannot. This is not to say Bath society was tolerant of the "loose" or "fast" but rather offered a more accepting eye to some things.

Society in Bath was considered deadly dull by some and a haven of genteel company without the fanatic glitter by others. It was possible to meet the residents in the Pump Room, on a promenade, or at the subscription balls in the upper rooms. The theater offered a pleasant diversion to all who wished to go.

One merely had to present his request to the master of ceremonies, and if not an outright scoundrel of monumental proportions, one would be accepted to join those events at the Upper Rooms.

This is not to suppose Phoebe or Claire would ever consider attending a ball in the New Assembly Rooms in their state of mourning. It would be quite acceptable, however, to take the healing waters, visit the Pump Room, or enjoy a Wednesday evening concert.

Gibbons's Bath agent had done well in selecting the charming house on Laura Street. Claire was delighted with its elegant comfort but went into raptures over the outstanding garden.

The pleasure of setting up the household held the charm of playing house for Claire. Claire moved from room to room in childish delight at her first "home." The fact that she did not consider Rosehill her home spoke volumes of her unhappiness while she lived there. This was different. This was *her* establishment!

She ordered fresh flowers every day and spent a happy hour arranging and shifting the bouquets. At Rosehill she had tended to the menus before and even did most of the cooking. Now Mrs. Harvey, the cook (the latest addition to her household was a kindly widow with a great deal of sympathy for Claire), cheerfully carried out her mistress's careful planning. And when the "family" gathered for dinner, it was a joyous occasion.

Tyndall watched with amusement as the ladies set about making the house exactly as they wished. He could not fault Claire for any extravagance. Her pleasure came from ordinary comforts, like cream for their coffee, fresh flowers to brighten the rooms, and cozy evenings together in the salon.

Claire continued to weave her story, for as soon as they settled in, she declared Eileen and Nathaniel were distant cousins on her mother's side. By doing so, she declared first names were appropriate. Phoebe agreed but worried at the growing number of falsehoods.

True to his promise, Tyndall came each day and instructed Claire in French. She would never be a master, for she did not have an ear for languages, but she would be proficient enough to get by in the salons of London. That was no real distinction, for some of the worst spoken French in the world occurred in glittering first circles.

This oddly assembled family slipped into a routine of genteel activity. Major Tyndall brought books to read and to discuss. He made every effort to approximate the salons of the first circles in topics of conversation. He introduced the art of the *on-dit*, which was the favorite pastime of society.

He introduced politics but warned that a "lady" for the most part avoided talking politics. It was considered a bit too bluestocking for most members of the ton. They discussed current events and showed her how to carefully weave gossip with politics. He introduced the attack on the Duke of Cumberland by his valet as a perfect example.

"I could understand wishing to throttle one's valet, but one must wonder why a valet would want to kill his master, especially if he was a royal duke," Claire said.

"You might have the answer if you knew the Duke of Cumberland," Tyndall said with a wry smile.

Claire laughed. She did so often in Nathaniel's company. She marveled at the ease with which he brought her from an untutored country girl to one who would soon be able to move among the highest sticklers.

She looked forward to his morning visits, and

when he did not feel well enough to come, she and Eileen worried excessively. Still, between Minton and Jamie, she knew he was in good hands.

"I think your health is much improved," Claire said when she noted his good color and lively spirit.

"Aye, and it's getting better since I've stopped that fool surgeon from bleeding me. I swear, it's a foul practice, and I am sure it does more harm than good; and I remain adamant on the subject. The doctor doesn't like it much, but little I care of that."

"I suppose you must know; however . . . ." Claire's voice trailed off, and she glanced toward Eileen. A look passed between them.

"No need to question the wisdom of it, you two. I know how I feel when I am not bled. He'll not get near me with a cup again, I assure you."

Claire did think he looked better, and one cannot argue with success. "I agree."

The days slipped by in quiet contentment. They shopped along Milsom Street, purchasing items for their London stay. They had several dresses made up in anticipation of their move to London. It was delicious fun to choose whatever one wished.

Claire was content, and a glow came to her countenance. The tired, drawn look faded as she gained some much-needed weight. Her new gowns and coiffure did wonders for her appearance and confidence. She began to carry the demeanor of a lady of means, stemming from not having to worry about the money for her next meal.

Phoebe even began to relax, for it seemed as

though their lies might not be found out. Perhaps Claire was doing the right thing after all, since she could not remember when they had been this happy. Claire continued to talk about all the wonderful things they would do, but it was the simple pleasures that were making her happy.

The quiet, pleasant days continued for weeks until Claire began to notice Eileen teasing Nathaniel to escort her to an assembly dance. While Eileen tried to hide her growing restlessness, it became more difficult with each passing week. They had done all the activities allowed, but Eileen was young and needed some young friends.

This occurred to Claire one evening when Eileen could not settle on any activity. She tossed her needlepoint aside.

"Eileen, should we play a parlor game?" Claire asked.

Eileen shook her head and tried to smile. They had played all the charades she would care to in a lifetime.

Claire could hear her sigh across the room. How foolish she had been to think a young lady would be content to tat every evening. She would speak to Nathaniel tomorrow. Perhaps he could take Eileen to an assembly dance. It could do no harm. But he could not dance and they had not yet made acquaintances to make up a party. It was time she made new friends. She realized she had become too complacent in the delight of this peaceful home.

Although this tranquil life was not what she had started out to pursue, she had no other option while in mourning. Just wait until we go to London, she thought; I will be rested, dressed to the nines, and ready to dance the night through.

To think on the subject further, she was sure the Dalton boys were homesick. While they would never admit it, she knew it was so. It was not wise for such active young men to be bored; they might begin looking for excitement in the wrong places. She had best send Will home before Christmas. Nate still needed Jamie.

Odd how nothing is ever really simple. She was now free and independent, and yet here were all these people dependent on her. So much for a carefree existence. Did one ever exist? For the first time a sense of restlessness swept her. Nothing was like she had thought it would be.

A frown played on her face a moment. She would dispense with such thinking. One step at a time. She was content with all that she had! An image of that arrogant aristocratic face flashed through her mind. She could almost feel his nearness. Her heart gave a wild flip and began to pound. Her cheeks flushed as her eyes widened. Where in heaven's name did that come from? She trembled and dismissed the thought quickly, for it was too unsettling and equally risky.

Glancing to Phoebe, then to Eileen, she could tell that neither had noticed her dismay. Thank goodness. She rose slowly, feigning a drowsiness that did not match her racing heart.

"I am turning in. Suddenly I am very tired. Come along, Eileen. Tomorrow we will see about making some acquaintances. I have been circumspect enough," Claire said, realizing she had best get other activities on her mind to keep a certain face from her thoughts.

"Good night, dear," Phoebe said. "I shall be going up in a moment, too."

Twelve

The Earl of Wentworth entered Hatchard's for what seemed to be the hundredth time in the singular hope of finding his elusive lady. *His* lady . . . Very much aware of his use of the possessive adjective, he shrugged.

Never had Lord Wentworth felt so thwarted and powerless. The dubious glances cast in his direction by the shopkeeper had almost put him to the blush, if such a thing could be conceived. His lordship actually took to smiling at the proprietor and purchased any number of volumes in the effort to put a reason for hanging around a bookseller's shop.

So as not to cause too much of an ado over his frequent appearances, he had set a man to watch the shop in hopes of the widow's return. That proved to be a disastrous effort when they chased down three different widows, none the one he was seeking. That endeavor was quickly abandoned, lest he be apprehended as a public nuisance. He could not give credence to his feeble attempts, the poor results, and his persistent search. Never had he acted so foolhardy. Nevertheless, he again found his steps taking him into the shop in which he had last seen her.

Quickly scanning the patrons, he was not surprised to see it was to no avail. Although several interested, feminine smiles greeted him, he paid them no heed. She was not here. Turning to leave, he knew full well he must forsake this folly.

It had been weeks since he had last seen her. It was obvious she had not remained in London. If he just knew where she came from. He had tried to find out. Having described her to as many people as he dared without raising a gossipy interest, he had received only blank stares. Finally he gave up asking, lest he be seen as a fool. He knew he was acting like a lovesick dolt; he need not advertise the fact.

Determined enough to be successful, he did not want anyone remembering his transparent interest in her. On affairs of the heart the less said or noted the better. Disappointment dogged his steps as he left the shop to saunter along the street.

The warmth that was early June reminded him he could linger no longer. It was late spring and he must return to Ireland. Enough time had been spent on looking for his mysterious lady. His business in London was finished; he could no longer put off returning to Dublin.

Retracing the route previously taken would offer the opportunity to question the innkeeper of the Royal Rose again. He had sent a Bow Street Runner for that purpose, but no information was uncovered. Bow Street Runners rarely failed, but, like all his ventures concerning the lady, this one came up negative. The innkeeper had claimed he could not remember the lady's name for she had never previously stayed there. Wentworth thought that unlikely.

Wentworth frowned. Perhaps not all sources had been tapped. The stablehands might remember the two husky young men who guarded her. Those lads may have mentioned to others where they were from or where they were headed. He brightened at this thought, even though it might prove to be his last chance.

Never, never had he given a fig for a face. He assumed that, as in most love affairs, this passion would burn itself out. After all, she was an ill-tempered vixen, for he had seen her in action. He smiled at the memory of the defiant lift of her chin and the challenge in her eyes, daring him. Such a companion would liven his lonely life, but he hoped it would soon become tiresome and he could return to his normal existence. He looked toward that event with almost as much anticipation as he looked forward to making love to this comely wench. She was far too distracting.

Squire Bradley had been shocked, annoyed, and wild with anger when he first learned of Claire Darington's sudden departure. By the devil's own hand, he had failed to call at Rosehill for a week after he offered for her. When he heard that a couple had been installed as caretakers, he had ridden over as fast as his horse could gallop.

Mr. and Mrs. Hampton were in possession of the house and, to make matters worse, were seeing to the renovation of the roof. Gardeners were cutting down overgrown bushes and cleaning beds. Bradley was stunned. How could this be?

He questioned the couple and received only the briefest reply: they were carrying out the mistress's orders. Bradley was furious and demanded to know where Miss Darington and Miss Greene had gone. Again he received a vague answer regarding a journey long desired and now taken. The whereabouts, of course, were completely unknown, as the mistress did not seek permission from them on where to travel. Bradley was then dismissed with the claim that there was much to do and they must get on with it.

In a blind fury, Bradley rode home. The following weeks only added to his frustration. Later he returned to Rosehill to find out where Claire had gone. Again no information was given. The upstart couple denied knowing any of their mistress's plans or whereabouts. She had not written them, and it would do no good if she had, for Mr. Hampton announced that neither of them could read. They sent Bradley on his way.

Bradley continued to chafe at the injustice of it all. The least the ungrateful Miss Darington could have done was to inform him of her departure. Had he not offered to marry her, to protect her and treat her with kindness? How ungrateful the wench was. No wonder Simon had ill-used her. She had probably provoked him with her hoity-toity ways. If she was ever in his power, he would make her pay for this indifferent treatment. The land. He thought of all that land. What were her intentions? He had to find her!

By June his anxiety had driven him so that now he found himself on the road to London on the theory that she had gone there.

The money was the mystery. Where did she get the money for the roof, the workmen, and the gardeners? That had been his power over her, for he was sure she was destitute. Was he mistaken? He smiled at the thought that there might be money and land, then frowned when he realized she would not accept him if she was financially independent. But it could not be much money . . . could it? These thoughts plagued his mind during the hours he spent on the road.

He asked at every inn from noon on if they remembered a lady of the description he offered. He found none who remembered seeing such a lady or her aunt. Mayhap they had not worn mourning, he thought. No, Claire would not fly in the face of propriety like that! Toward evening he was tired and every bone in his body ached from the poor springs of his old traveling coach. When they reached Grantham, he ordered his coachman to pull into the Royal Rose. It seemed a likely place.

With a pang of envy he noted a fine crested coach entering the courtyard. He used his so seldom; it did not behoove him to purchase a new one, but today he had paid the price for that economy. Stiffly alighting from the coach, he brushed his traveling coat, checked his neck cloth, and headed toward the entrance of the inn.

"I need a room for the night. Show me the taproom; I'm as dry as the Sahara. I hope your bill of fare is worth its boast posted on your sign."

The innkeeper bowed. "Aye, we are known for the fine victuals served here. Nobles and gentries alike stop here. They do that." He continued bowing, all the while showing his stained teeth in a wide, fawning smile. He directed Squire Bradley to a table by the glowing fire in the large taproom. The spring evening was taking on a chill.

Bradley nodded approval and took a seat. "Bring me a tankard of ale before I perish. By the by, were there two ladies in mourning traveling through here about six weeks ago? One was old and the other young and exceedingly handsome," Bradley told the innkeeper as a barmaid brought the tankard of ale.

At that moment the inn door opened and a party of aristocrats entered. Noting them, the proprietor offered his excuses and left the squire sitting with his unanswered question. Bradley frowned, but then he could see the richly dressed gentleman and his entourage enter the hall of the inn. He could hardly fault the landlord for his obsequious manner. Money was money. He would ask again. He turned his thoughts to the meal, took a sip of ale, and relaxed.

* * *

"Good evening, your lordship. We are honored you have returned to us. I will have the room that was so rudely denied you the last time," the innkeeper said, and bowed. He straightened with a perplexed expression and looked toward the taproom. "I wonder if he is asking about that widow who nabbed your room when last you were here. Seems to be about six weeks. Was it six weeks since ye be here?"

The Earl of Wentworth raised an eyebrow and glanced toward the taproom. "Yes, exactly six weeks."

"Odd that the man should be asking after them," the innkeeper said. "Never the mind." He snapped his fingers, sending a maid to escort Nanny Rourke and Julie to a room next to his lordship's. "I'll have a meal sent to them shortly. My lord, you'll be wanting the private parlor," he said, and headed in that direction.

The earl paused and looked into the half-filled taproom. He spied a country gentleman sitting by the fire, enjoying his tankard of ale. "No, I think I will take my supper in here tonight." His lordship entered the taproom and took a chair not far from the country squire, sending him a nod.

The squire returned the nod and sat a little taller as he pulled in his stomach. His attire must not look too countrified. The thought pleased him as he again adjusted his neck cloth. But the sartorial splendor of the dark-haired gentleman was far above his touch. He supposed Claire would fancy such a handsome fellow, and the idea did not please him. He had better find Claire before she took a fancy to someone else.

The earl turned to the squire. "Do you find the food here good?"

"Never had the occasion to eat here before," the squire replied.

"I have done so once, and I found it to be quite passable. I am sure your cook provides much better, but then on the road we are to be considered fortunate if we aren't poisoned," the earl said confidentially, intimating he considered the squire on an equal footing. Wentworth had an uncanny ability to read a man, and it seldom disappointed him. This evening was no different. Squire Bradley fell into a smug feeling of comradery with this aristocratic lord.

The earl ordered a bottle of claret and asked what was on the evening menu. His ruby signet ring flashed on his hand, as did the diamond in his cravat pin. He then turned to Bradley and introduced himself. "I am the Earl of Wentworth."

"Squire Bradley here, and I am proud to make your acquaintance." He took a swig of ale.

"Come this way often?" the earl asked.

"No, no, my estates keep me far too busy to be roving about the countryside."

"I can well imagine," the earl replied.

The innkeeper bustled in with maids carrying two trays piled with assorted dishes. The servants busied themselves with the placing of dishes on each table. It did smell good, and the earl nodded with approval.

The meal consisted of roast chicken, sliced ham smothered with gravy, and new potatoes. The two gentlemen ate in silence, but the earl directed a question or two to the country squire. The meal was ample and good. Both sat back refreshed when the innkeeper came in to see if all was to their liking.

"Did you think on the question I asked you?" Squire Bradley asked the proprietor.

"Question?"

"Yes, if two ladies, one old, the other young—in mourning they were—came here about six weeks ago."

"No ... well, yea. There were two widows that stayed here. You remember, my lord. They was widows."

"No, these aren't widows. They are spinsters, or at least the older one is. Although the younger one could be considered a spinster, too, for all her age," the squire said.

"Then it weren't them two. They was widows. You remember," the innkeeper said, and turned to his lordship.

His lordship flourished a yawn. "Can't say that I do. Bring me some port and clear the plates. Would you join me in some port, squire? Tell me, how is hunting around here during the season? This is your home area?"

"No, Yorkshire. Aye, be honored to join you for

a bit of port." He rose and crossed over to his lordship's table.

"So, you are from Yorkshire?"

"Aye, I am Squire Bradley of Thornten."

"I am not much familiar with that part of England. I have passed through the region, of course, but never stayed there. I reside in Dublin most of the year. I have been in London for Parliament and now head home," the earl said, much against his natural inclination. He never spoke of personal matters to anyone. It annoyed him now to curry this fat, pompous squire's favor. He shrugged his fine shoulders—any port in a storm, he thought.

"You now come from London?"

"Aye."

Squire Bradley muttered that he was bound for that hellhole, much to his distaste.

"Why go? Or must you go for business?"

"I go to seek my intended."

"My felicitations. So you marry a London lass?"

"Nay. She lives in Yorkshire; her lands march next to mine. Rosehill, it is, and a pitiful place indeed. Good land, though, and I mean to have it." The squire spoke more to himself than to the earl, and his brown eyes glittered with malice as he took a deep swig of wine.

Hackles rose on the back of Wentworth's neck. The ominous message hidden in the squire's voice shouted warning.

"Gone to get her bride clothes, I take it. Cost her father a pretty penny, I bet," the earl said, hoping against hope to draw him out. Could Bradley's "in tended" be the same beauty he sought? Never, she would not have the likes of this bully.

Wentworth filled the squire's glass again.

"Not likely. That bastard died over two months ago. It weren't timely, neither. He promised me Claire, and I mean to have her."

"Claire?"

Bradley finished his glass and poured another. He sent a wrenching belch throughout the room and downed the glass again.

"Aye, Claire, Claire Darington. A contrary beauty and I mean to have her." He slurred his words slightly as he repeated his claim. "If only she had consented before old Simon stuck his spoon in the wall. The bastard up and died, just when I was about to get her consent."

"Tragic, now you have to wait till her mourning is over." The earl quickly counted that to be in about nine or ten months.

The squire snorted. "The land marches next to mine. Simon promised me the land if I relinquished her dowry."

"Would you relinquish her dowry?"

"Hell, yes. There ain't no money there. Couldn't be. Simon gambled it away years ago. He's been selling off the furniture and plates these last ten years."

"If the land is good, I suppose one might dispense with a dowry," Wentworth said.

"Exactly my sentiments. But the wench hired on caretakers and took off with that mealymouthed aunt of hers and without a by-your-leave. How's that for gratitude?"

"Shocking. Left without saying good-bye to her own betrothed. What is this younger generation coming to?" the earl said, and smiled a smile that was contrary to the glitter in his eyes.

Thirteen

$\mathcal{G}$ray clouds swept across the sky, driving rain in gusts of pelting spikes that came in varying waves of intensity. Claire stood fascinated, watching the splashing water that formed rivulets and trailed along the cobbled road. The weather had been dreary for weeks.

The damp was chilling, despite the merry fire. Claire tucked her shawl around her and returned to the cozy chair by the hearth. "Not fit for man or beast," she mumbled.

Phoebe nodded as she drew out her needle from the dainty embroidery she was working on.

"It is good that we sent Will home. Think how confined he would feel," Claire said.

"Yes, I think Jamie would have liked to go, too, but Nathaniel still needs him. I admire his willingness to remain with Nate. Shows character. They are good lads."

"That they are. I have to admit, I shall miss the comfort of knowing a strong man is at hand," Claire replied.

Phoebe nodded. "He will be back after harvest.

Besides, idle hands can lead a lad to lark about. I fear that is what is wrong with half the young men of the first circles."

"Well, that is one less worry. Who would have thought my freedom would pose so many responsibilities? For example, our life is far lacking in entertainment for Eileen. I fear she, too, is bored by the thin company we share in Bath. Perhaps London will be more interesting."

"Claire, you know it will. Besides, Eileen is not your responsibility. She is Nate's. He puts far too much on you, I fear. I do not like to speak unkindly, but it's the truth."

"Nate cannot get about very well. Can you imagine him spending hours poring over fabrics and laces? Besides, I have enjoyed adding them to my life. Nate has been so valuable to me. Look at all that I have learned. If I may boast a bit, I do not think one might discern that all my years were spent buried in the country."

"I agree. You look and act as though you've lived in Bath most of your life. I am very proud of you, my dear. You are a credit to me. I just hope London is all you hope it will be."

"It will be. I needed this time in Bath to rest, learn, and cream my hands." A dimple appeared at the corner of her mouth, and her eyes danced merrily as she held out her soft white hands to admire them.

Perkins, the butler, entered and announced, "A visitor is calling and wishes to speak with Miss Darington. He insisted on seeing the 'lady of the house' when I informed him there is no Miss Dar ington at this address."

"Has he given his name?" Claire asked as a sof pink colored her cheeks.

"A Mr. Ian O'Mara, madam," Perkins replied somehow managing to cast a look that was flat ye speculative simultaneously.

Claire glanced toward Phoebe, who nodded. "Bes to see, dear."

"Send him in, Perkins."

Within seconds a lithe, small man entered. He was well dressed, though modestly so. His skin was that of one who spent a great deal of time in the open. His eyes were blue and merry, and deep smile lines radiated out from his eyes.

"Ian O'Mara, madam, at your service. I do hope I am not intruding. I come as instructed by a friend on a rather surprising mission." O'Mara waited un til Perkins departed; then he checked the hall and returned to the center of the room.

This struck Claire as extremely odd behavior, and she became alarmed. If only Will were still but a call away.

"State your business, and just who is the friend?"

He cleared his throat. "Miss Darington, I am to inform you that Squire Bradley is now on his way to Bath."

"Squire Bradley is on his way to Bath?"

"Aye, it seems he is most desirous of finding Miss Darington. I have been sent to warn you so that you can take whatever steps you might wish to avoid him."

Claire's mouth hung open in utter amazement. Phoebe gasped as she brought her fingers to her lips.

"Who are you?" Claire asked incredulously.

"I am the horse trainer and groom at Rosehill. I learned from Will Dalton that Squire Bradley was on his way. Bradley inadvertently learned of your stay in Bath when he was looking over the new mounts. It was a mere slip of the tongue. Will was abashed the minute he let it out. It went no further. The squire knows only that you are in Bath, nothing else."

"What new mounts?" Claire was on her feet. "Head groomsman at Rosehill? Who hired you?"

O'Mara offered a thoroughly beguiling smile that was all innocent charm. "Don't rightly know his name. A gentleman from London hired me on behalf of the owner of Rosehill. Been there since summer. I might add, you will be pleased with the stables and the quality of your horses." O'Mara shifted and watched under hooded eyes for her reaction.

"Gibbons must have done so," she said to Phoebe. "How very odd. I gave him no such orders."

O'Mara did not like the avenue her thoughts were taking. He hastily added, "You'll be pleased at the roof on the manor. The gardens are coming about, too. Not like it must have been, but by next summer they will be outstanding. You must see for yourself all the excellent improvements about the manor and grounds."

"I see. How odd. You say you came from Rosehill.

How much of a head start to the squire did you have?"

"Can't say to that. I ... er ... came immediately after Will mentioned Bath. Have I done wrong?"

"No, no. It is all ... well ... never mind. Thank you for informing me. You were right to do so. I have no intention of seeing Squire Bradley. Does he know I am a widow now?"

"No, I was there at the time. That fool squire pops up at Rosehill, out of nowhere, always sniffing about. He was set on finding your whereabouts. Will was mightily disturbed at letting it slip. He said nothing else, knowing your instructions not to let anyone know of your stay. The lad understands that is so the squire don't know where you are and come apestering you. That is why I came straightaway."

"You are correct. Thank you for the information. It does give me the warning I need. Are you returning to Rosehill?"

"Yes, if it is what you wish. I thought I was hired to restore the stables and take care of the horses. That is what you wish?"

"Yes, of course. My man of business has done this, thinking it necessary. Do carry on."

"I will keep me ears and eyes open, madam. Bradley does not know I have ridden to Bath. I came straightaway. He went for a good night's sleep first before he started out." O'Mara's eyes twinkled.

Wentworth's faith in the man was not unfounded. O'Mara had easily slipped into the daily life at Rosehill. In little time he became a trusted member of the staff and gleaned every piece of in

122

formation he could. He served Wentworth first, and Miss Darington second, but he had trembled when she questioned him about his hiring. He was glad when she assumed it was *her* man of business who had done so.

This was a damnable foolish business. He did not understand it. Fortunately he had learned the name of her man of business, a Mr. Gibbons. His lordship might want to know that name. What this was all about he had not fathomed, that is, until he saw her. His curiosity about his mission disappeared the minute he laid eyes on the fair Miss Darington.

O'Mara bowed and excused himself. "I will return to Rosehill come morning. I stay at the Swan. If you wish me to carry any instructions, please let me know."

He wondered why she had not volunteered her new name. He had not asked. Instinctively he knew she still wished her whereabouts unknown to the staff at Rosehill. She obviously had good reasons, with the tiresome squire so determined to find her. First he thought it must be the land, but after seeing her, he knew it had to be more.

Leaving the salon and crossing the hall to pick up his hat and gloves, he spied a letter addressed to Mrs. Anseley. He left the house. It was now his turn to be shocked. Mrs. Anseley, her name was Mrs. Anseley! No wonder his lordship was interested in the lovely lady.

This was the queerest mission he had ever taken for the earl. Why would Lord Wentworth want to spy on a lady who was obviously connected to him?

* * *

The peace and pleasure of Bath had been shattered. Within minutes trunks were hauled out.

"Just the necessary items for now, Dora. Pack the rest to follow up to London later," Claire ordered.

She found Perkins looking pale and confused. "No need to worry, Perkins, you did right by letting Mr O'Mara in. The man has done me a service. I do not want to see my former suitor."

"Madam, he would not get past me!"

"Oh, I know that. But I have no intention of hiding in my own home lest I run into that fortune hunter!" Claire spoke frankly, for Perkins must understand why she was rushing to London.

"Call Fields to bring around the coach in an hour. You and Dora will follow as soon as the packing is completed."

Claire rushed to tell the cook to prepare a basket of food.

"Oh, Phoebe, I wish Will were back! Eileen, go get your brother and Jamie."

Tyndall arrived within minutes of his summons. "Do not worry, Claire. I'll see the house closed. Jamie and I will follow within a week. I'll see that O'Mara fellow sends Will to you in London. You say he is at the Swan. Jamie, go tell him to send Will to London."

Claire nodded, grateful that Nathaniel was there to see to the house.

"I shall remain until after the squire comes, in case he hangs around a while to spy on who comes and goes. If he shows up on this doorstep, I shall act as though he is loony. Never heard of a Miss Darington! If he asks about in Bath, no one else will either. They know you as Mrs. Anseley; they will not connect the two names. He will not be able to find you. Take Dora; you will have need of her."

"Oh, Nate, I knew I could depend on you! What would we do without you? Yes, you are correct. Bradley will lose the trail here," Claire said.

Exactly one hour later Phoebe, Eileen, Claire, and Dora climbed into the coach. Fields cracked the whip, and they were headed for London.

Fourteen

The gray drizzle of the dark winter day was such as to keep inhabitants indoors. A stay-at-home-and hibernate day. Not immune to the dictates of weather, Claire sat with Aunt Phoebe before the hearth, enjoying the dancing flames and the warmth sent into the cozy room.

They had done little else since their premature departure from Bath. The unexpected arrival of Squire Bradley in Bath had sent Claire and her "family" fleeing to London.

She had not wanted to stand up against the squire, which, of course, is what she should have done. The reason was that she did not want him to know she was now a "widow." No telling what trouble he could cause with that piece of information. The results of the flight weighed heavily on Claire. Was it only a matter of time? Was the masquerade worth it? She began to doubt her decision.

Although they now sat comfortably by the fire, the flight from Bath had unnerved her and the hurried establishing of this house had been too hectic. Servants had been hastily hired and her household established. So they now sat resting by the fire to soothe their frazzled nerves.

Claire and Phoebe looked up when Perkins entered and announced, "Madam, the Earl of Wentworth calls. He wishes to speak with you." Looking very smart in his crimson-and-gold livery, Perkins appeared very placid, as if earls called every day. Since they had received no visitors, Claire marveled at his loftiness.

Claire glanced toward Phoebe, who gave a slight nod.

"Send him up, Perkins, and see that tea and refreshments are served."

"Very good, Madam." He bowed and left the room to fetch the Earl of Wentworth.

Claire felt her cheeks flush and her heart set off in a gallop. "Phoebe, whatever is he doing here? How in heavens did he learn we are here? And whatever for?" Claire cried.

"How could I possibly know, dear?" A singularly novel idea crossed her mind. "But we shall soon see."

"The Earl of Wentworth," Perkins announced in lofty fashion, as the tall, admirable earl crossed the threshold into the sitting room.

Claire thought he looked exceedingly handsome and immediately raised her guard even further. She hated people who traded on their looks. Where she got the idea that he traded on his looks was nowhere to be found; she just assumed it. Anyone that handsome and that arrogant must do so.

He wore a superbly cut coat that fitted his broad

shoulders as close as wall covering on a wall. The coat was of blue, superfine cloth, his trousers of a soft beige, and his neck cloth a precisely folded Oriental.

He crossed the room and bowed over Aunt Phoebe's hand. "Miss Greene, I hope I find you well." When he looked into Phoebe's eyes, she almost gasped at the merriment in them. She returned his smile. What else could one do? He invoked the smile. And while she might be an elderly lady, she was not dead yet. The man fairly oozes charm, she mused. How will Claire handle this accomplished gentleman? The question lit a merry twinkle in her blue eyes.

Next he crossed to Claire and bowed over her hand. "I hope you are also in the bloom of good health. But then I can see that is so." Claire met his eyes, and her heart nearly jumped from her chest. There was fire in his eyes, smoldering flame that reached out and seared her. She trembled and withdrew her hand.

"Please be seated, your lordship."

He obeyed, taking the corner on the settee next to Claire, and crossed his long legs, which were ensconced in elegant Hessian boots. He appeared completely at home, as though he had sat in this room often.

"I come to offer an apology for the unfortunate incident at the Royal Rose. I offer the excuse that I was not aware of the situation, for it seems the proprietor was trying to cater to too many people at the same time."

"You need not have gone to such trouble to make this apology. The incident is long past and long forgotten. How did you find us?"

"Find you, Mrs. Anseley? Were you lost?"

Claire frowned at him and clenched a fist. She knew she was right! The man *is* high and mighty!

Phoebe saw Claire's dangerous expression and quickly spoke. "What my niece means is, how did you find us here in London?"

"Find you? Actually, I was not looking for you, but happened to see your . . . er . . . rather formidable retainer. One is not likely to forget those robust retainers. Of course, I did see you in Hatchard's, but you failed to recognize me, Mrs. Anseley."

Claire shifted a bit. He was making her feel most uncomfortable. Damnation! This is my home! The nerve of the man. He would not get away with it!

She offered a dazzling smile. "I am afraid I do not remember seeing you at Hatchard's. In fact, I would not have known you, had Perkins not announced you. How is your dear daughter? Staying safely under caring eyes, I hope." She smiled a condescending smile.

Wentworth cocked an eyebrow. He would watch out for that dazzling smile; it seemed to bode a coming setdown. His lips twitched, and he committed her face again to memory. She was more beautiful than he remembered, and still as contentious.

His eyes lit with amusement, which offended Claire. "You are amused, sir?"

His insouciance disappeared in an instant. He sat

129

upright. "Not amused, only charmed. I come with the fervent request that you and Miss Greene accompany me to the opera tomorrow evening. It is a small token to offer as the apology I apparently have failed to convey. I would not see you uncomfortable for all the kingdoms of this world." His eyes still reflected humor.

"A pretty speech, indeed." Claire repressed a smile, for his manner and charm inexplicably touched her. Dropping her eyes, she toyed with the ribbons that cascaded down from below her bodice.

At that moment the door opened, and the butler entered with the tea cart. The tangy smell of fresh tarts mingled with the sweet scones and Ceylon tea.

Claire took up the teapot and a cup and saucer. "Tea, Lord Wentworth?"

He nodded as she passed the first cup to Aunt Phoebe and began to pour the second. His eyes lingered on her face. The soft rose color she wore reflected a soft pink in her cheeks, unless he had put the blush there. Not likely, he thought, she does not even like me. He shrugged. She did not know him. He would change that.

His eyes lingered on her soft mouth and traveled the length of her body, taking in every detail. She was beautifully dressed in an exquisite gown made by a master. Her hands were soft and white, and she moved with elegant grace.

The door flew open and in bounded Eileen, followed by Major Tyndall. "Claire, wait until you see what Nate has—Oh, pardon me. I did not know you had company."

The child always bounded. When would she learn she must enter as a lady? Claire wondered. She must speak to her again.

Claire made the introductions.

Wentworth had risen at Eileen's entrance. After shaking hands with Major Tyndall, he retook his seat. Surveying the handsome young major, he sent a questioning look to Claire. The slightest frown flittered across his eyes and disappeared as quickly as it had come. She smiled at Tyndall with an intimacy that struck Wentworth's heart with terror.

The young man presented a romantic picture— the wounded hero. What lady could resist that? For the first time in his life, Wentworth experienced doubt about his ability to woo and win a lady. Competition from another man had never, ever entered his mind.

"I have come to beg Mrs. Anseley and Miss Greene to join in a party for the opera tomorrow evening. Will you and your sister join us?" the earl asked, his fine eyes resting easily on the Tyndalls. The best way to eliminate a rival was to meet him head-on, Wentworth thought. The major would understand more than most: there is no defense like an offense.

Eileen's enthusiasm burst forth. "How famous! Claire, isn't that just famous? Why, only yesterday you said you were bored and desperate for some entertainment. You will say yes?" Eileen beamed from ear to ear, waiting patiently for Claire's answer.

All eyes turned to Claire. Phoebe's twinkled with

mischief. How will she wiggle out of this one, if indeed she wants to.

Nathaniel watched Claire, noting the heightened color of her cheeks. He glanced again at Wentworth. Where did she know *him* from? He frowned, wanting to say they were otherwise engaged for the evening.

Claire blushed even deeper as all sat awaiting her reply. She would sound foolish to say no. After all, she had, until this moment, been bored beyond tears. They had been nowhere. Her glittering social life had not even begun! She could wear her new apricot silk.

"You are too kind. Yes, we shall all be delighted to join you tomorrow for an evening at the opera."

"You honor me."

She met his gaze frankly. "It will be a much welcomed event. We have long been confined." She wanted him to know the "event" was what attracted them, not him!

"I am gratified to see you enjoying some of the delights London has to offer. Life is for the living. I am sure you agree."

Aunt Phoebe, Major Tyndall, and Claire stared at Wentworth with one thought: he was extremely presumptuous.

"Yes! That is exactly my thought," Eileen said. "I am so glad, for you see, I shall make my come-out this spring."

Claire's fingers went to her lips. When next she talked to Eileen about bounding into a room, she would forcibly mention to keep her mouth shut!

She did not want Lord Wentworth to know too much about her. Still, *she* had accepted him as escort for an evening's entertainment. Why?

Phoebe and Eileen had sat on their seats so expectantly, with eager expressions on their faces. What else could she have done? She was annoyed with them and herself.

Still, she did want to get about, to meet members of society, and what better way than on the arm of an earl? She blushed at this calculating thought. Surely she was above taking advantage of someone to gain admittance into society's hallowed portals! She dismissed the idea with the justifying thought that she had agreed to his suggestion before any such thought occurred to her. She was not an opportunist! That was considerably different from seizing an opportunity, and an earl would be elevating in the eyes of the ton.

With a start, she realized the earl had spoken and was waiting for a reply. Her musings had led her away from the surrounding conversation.

"I beg your pardon. I did not hear what you said."

Wentworth was taken aback for the second time. She had not even been listening! He shifted. Perhaps it was time to take his leave. He placed his cup on the table.

"Please repeat what you said. I confess; I was wool-gathering." She smiled apologetically.

His lips twitched in a hovering smile, and once again amusement shone from his eyes. So much for my captivating conversation, he thought.

" 'Tis of no importance. I must bid my farewell.

I have a small business matter to attend to." He started to rise.

"He wanted to know if your husband was military, and if he perished on the Peninsular," Phoebe interjected. She waited, fascinated, to hear Claire's reply.

"Yes. He was wounded and died in Portugal." She lowered her eyes and blushed to her roots.

"Richard died in my arms. A braver man does not exist," Tyndall hastily added. A growing, ominous feeling concerning the earl crept over him.

"Richard Anseley died in your arms?"

"Aye, and it was a sad day, I tell you. He was an honorable man and my good friend."

The earl's jaw muscles tightened and an ashen, grave expression hardened his features. "Had you been married long?"

Claire trembled. "Only a very short time," she whispered.

"I am acquainted with a family in Ireland named Anseley. I wonder if they are connected?"

"Heavens, no!" Phoebe squeaked.

Her distress is too obvious, Claire thought.

Major Tyndall's mouth opened and closed. He did not speak.

Eileen sat, waiting for Claire to say something.

"Perhaps," Claire coolly replied. "I know little of his family. Richard was estranged from them. For reasons of our own, we kept our marriage a secret."

"Indeed."

"Indeed, sir. But, as you can imagine, this is all too painful. May we speak of something else?" She offered a poignant expression and turned to Tyndall.

The earl rose. "I would be honored if you would join me for dinner one evening, Major Tyndall."

"Be delighted."

Wentworth turned to the ladies. "Good day to you all. Until tomorrow evening." He gave a slight bow and moved to leave. "Please, I shall see my way out. I know this house well. I am a friend of Lord Swarthfield, your landlord."

The second the front door closed, they all began to speak.

"How did he find us? Why did he go out of his way to find us? Do you suppose he suspects?" Claire asked.

"Suspects what?" Nathaniel asked.

"About my widowhood! He brought it up."

"My dear, it was a natural topic. He was only trying to be polite. After all, the last time he saw you, you were in widow weeds," Aunt Phoebe said.

"But why seek me out?" Claire wailed.

Silence again fell, with all eyes turned on Claire.

"My gracious, Cousin Claire. I am not even out and can recognize a smitten swain. You are old; you should, too!"

"Enough, Eileen," Nathaniel said, raising his hand to caution his impulsive sister.

"*Smitten?* I doubt that! He is devilishly highhanded. I doubt he is smitten by anyone but himself." Claire gave an emphatic nod of her head as if to settle that.

"Cousin Claire, you're mad. He is divine. Did you

ever see such gorgeous eyes? He could not take them off you! I swear, the man is besotted," Eileen exclaimed.

"Enough, Eileen." Nathaniel rose, looking more than a little pale. Suddenly he was not feeling too well. He cast a glance toward Claire, but she was not looking his way. She was too caught up in her own thoughts. A frown creased his brow.

"I intend to call on Lady Compton tomorrow. Perhaps she knows a bit about the man. I shall be discreet, of course. It is my hope that she will sponsor vouchers for Eileen at Almack's." His voice sounded far more cheerful than he felt.

"Shall I call tomorrow?" he asked.

Claire looked up. "Yes, of course. Are you not staying for dinner?"

"No. I must run along. Eileen, you behave yourself!" Tyndall forced a smile, then left the room. A deep frown furrowed his brow.

Fifteen

It was no easy task to appear calm while waiting for the day to pass into evening. Claire was eager to go to the opera to see and be seen. At last her life was beginning!

She hummed a little tune throughout the day and even marveled at her ebullience. It was such fun to think of the beautiful apricot silk gown that hung waiting with all the carefully chosen accessories. It was perfect.

Not even the disconcerting earl could dampen her perpetual smile. She simply would not let his penetrating eyes unnerve her. After all, he was a mere widower himself.

She bit her lip at her easy acceptance of her fabrication. He was a *real* widower. Still, she had lived the story for close to a year and had almost come to believe it herself. She shrugged. This was an opportunity, and she was seizing it. All her life she had dreamed of having just such a moment. Now it was reality. Surely the handsome lord, despite the fact that he was an odious creature, would lend her distinction. She spread her arms and danced around the room. Delicious, how very delicious life was.

The apricot dress did all that was promised. She stood before the mirror, pleased as a cat with a bowl of cream. Turning this way and that, she nodded approval at her appearance.

"You look perfect," Dora declared, as delighted as her mistress at the vision of beauty that stood before her. After all, she had arranged that wonderful cascade of ringlets, skillfully falling over each ear.

Phoebe rustled into the room in her pearl taffeta, looking very fine indeed. "Claire, I have never seen you lovelier. The dress becomes you." She smiled with loving satisfaction at seeing her niece blooming in the beauty of happiness.

"Aunt Phoebe, you look beautiful. The epitome of the fashionable woman," Claire declared, and kissed her sweet aunt on her cheek.

Eileen next appeared at the door, looking as pretty as any young lady of seventeen can hope to. She wore a soft white gown trimmed in lace and tied with blue ribbons. Matching ribbons were woven through her hair with little forget-me-nots. She was as charming and fresh as an April morning.

Claire and Phoebe gave her praise and hugs. She stood beaming with the first understanding of what it is to be a woman and one in the beginning of her beauty.

When the ladies descended the staircase, they

were met by Major Tyndall and the Earl of Wentworth. Both men looked up with appreciation.

Greetings were exchanged, and Claire thought the earl and Nathaniel looked marvelously handsome. Her stomach fluttered with butterflies, but she tried to pose a cool, elegant air. Whether she was successful or not she did not know. She was very much aware that the earl's eyes found hers frequently.

When they entered King's Theater, Claire tried not to marvel too openly at the splendor of the interior. Five tiers of seating boxes rose almost to the ceiling. The large dome had an illusionary painting of the classical gods of mythology traversing the sky in chariots.

The audience was large in anticipation of the presentation of Sidageo by Gughelini. She took in the beautifully gowned ladies and their sparkling jewels. It seemed as though Wentworth's party was attracting as much interest as his party returned.

Eileen's enthusiasm spilled over, and Claire secretly wished she could express her delight as openly. She smiled with Eileen's excitement, and her eyes met the earl's. He returned the smile in some kind of understanding. Claire quickly turned to the rising curtain. Could he read her thoughts? Of course not! Then why did she get the impression he could?

Signor Tranezzani strutted the stage as he sang the tragic tale. Signora Collini and Mme. Calderine, whose voice was exceptional, performed to the pleasure of the audience. There were no heckling catcalls or mooing cows to express disapproval of the performance. The audience clapped with appreciation.

Claire's eyes glowed with happiness. Wentworth sat back, half in shadow, and allowed his gaze to rest often on the lovely Mrs. Anseley.

She was an enigma, he thought. The air of innocence did not match her situation. She was accomplished, beautiful, and gave a hint of independence. Still, a mystery surrounded her. Had she been married to his nephew, Richard? He could hardly ask for a marriage certificate. But Richard had spent his leave in Dublin before his departure to the Peninsular. When would he have married?

He was drawn to her beyond anything he had known. If she had been Richard's wife, he could hardly offer carte blanche, which had been his beginning intention. Not even he knew now just what his intention was.

Shrugging, he noticed Major Tyndall watching him. And just where in the hell did this "warrior hero" fit in, he wondered with a derisive smile. For the life of him, he could not tell how Claire regarded this handsome rival. There was an intimacy between them that he could not fathom, at least on Mrs. Anseley's part. Perhaps it was friendship, but that could very well be his hopeful projection. He held no such doubt on Major Tyndall's feelings. The man was in love with her. He turned his eyes to the stage.

The second performance was a dance depicting

the emperor and empress of Russia and the pasha of Turkey. The dancer, Angiolini, amazed the audience by dancing on point for half an hour.

"Mrs. Anseley, the audience has been most kind this evening. I have known them to taunt the entertainers off the stage for lack of an acceptable performance." Wentworth had leaned over and whispered in her ear.

Claire turned in surprise. "I should think that would be so lowering as to drive them from ever performing again."

"No, actors seem to have elephant hides. No amount of criticism could drive a true performer from his art. I suppose they might very well pass it off as some perceived lack of appreciation for true artistic value," Wentworth said, and softly chuckled.

"All a matter of perspective, I should think," she said with a merry smile that brought the tiny dimple by the side of her mouth.

"Exactly. It always comes down to one's perspective."

What did he mean by "it"? she wondered. "My lord, are you a philosopher?"

He chuckled. "No, only an interested observer of human nature. I might add that not all the thespian skills are on the stage this night. Do you agree?"

Claire snapped open her fan and turned her attention to the stage. She leaned and whispered something to Major Tyndall. She never again turned back to look at Wentworth until the last curtain fell.

Wentworth's party waited for his carriage to be brought forward. They squeezed in as before, with the gentlemen facing back on the first seat and the three ladies facing forward.

Eileen chatted merrily, and Claire joined in when asked a direct question. Aunt Phoebe went on to discuss the merits of the opera, and the gentlemen nodded or added a brief comment. The tension ran high in that temporary, closed little world.

Claire watched the pools of light from the flickering street lamps and the dim glow that filled the carriage from time to time. The intimacy of the close quarters seemed to press in on Claire. She kept her eyes averted and continued to watch the passing scene.

Wentworth escorted the ladies to the door. "Good night. I cannot remember when I enjoyed an evening more." Bowing over Claire's hand, he took it to his lips.

"Mrs. Anseley, would you allow me to escort you to some of London's interesting sights?"

Claire bit her lower lip. She wanted to say yes, but he was so threatening. Precisely how, she was not sure, except to say that he had the charm of Lucifer.

"Perhaps, but the weather has been so inclement. . . ." Her voice trailed away. She raised her eyes to his.

He looked down. Amusement shone like green fire.

"Inclement weather? Mrs. Anseley, you strike me as a lady who would not let a little weather inhibit an outing. Am I to assume you would rather I did not call? If so, please say so."

Claire marveled at his frank speech and the humor that faded from his eyes. Aghast at his words, she placed her hand on his arm. "Your lordship, I meant no such thing."

His hand covered hers. "Then may I call again?"

"Please do." She turned to enter the foyer.

"Mrs. Anseley, speak only the truth to me." His voice was low, and she could not be sure she had heard him correctly.

Claire stood in the foyer when the door had closed, with flaming cheeks and glittering eyes. That awful man! What did he mean?

Eileen skipped happily up the stairs. "Claire, the man is divine. Oh, how I wish I were older, or he younger, or you in India." She giggled and tossed off an air kiss. "Good night. Sweet dreams, Claire."

Claire grabbed Phoebe's arm when they reached the top of the stairs and dragged her into the library.

"He knows. He knows. I know he knows!" Claire cried.

"Knows what?" Phoebe asked, with a sinking heart.

"That I am a fraud!"

"How could he? What makes you say so?"

"He told me to speak only the truth to him!" Claire waited for her revelation to sink in.

"He must have referred to the stupid answer you

148

gave him saying you couldn't go out in bad weather. He was surely offended by that weak excuse. It is almost as bad as saying you could not go out because you had to water your plants. Really, Claire."

Claire looked surprised. "You may be right. That did sound like I was avoiding him. I did not mean that. He is so very disconcerting. I felt overwhelmed by the man. He's . . . so . . ."

"Masculine?"

"Yes, yes, exactly. Do you agree?"

"Indeed, and I wish I were younger. I would hope he would overwhelm me."

"Aunt Phoebe!"

Phoebe put her hand on her niece's shoulder and directed her steps toward her bedchamber. "Go to bed, child. Sleep. We shall talk about the man tomorrow."

Claire obeyed. But she did not sleep, and she did not wait until tomorrow to think about him. The Earl of Wentworth plagued her waking hours and troubled her sleeping dreams. She tossed and turned.

Drat the man! She did not want any entanglements. She wanted to have fun, to dance, to ride, to . . . His green eyes came to mind and a thrill ran through her. Just as it had done when he so rudely held her that day in the courtyard.

That was it! He was dangerous. He sent her pulses racing. What it would be like to be covered by his kisses . . . Great Scott! She had come to London to have some adventure and was well on her way to becoming a wanton. She must dispense with such thoughts.

Squire Bradley drove her away because he was too repulsive. Wentworth frightened her away because he was too exciting. She needed a safe, nondescript man. No, she needed no man!

Sixteen

Several days later Lady Compton received Major Tyndall with a great show of pleasure. "How grand to see you, and to see you so well. Come, join us," she said, rising to his entrance into her blue salon. "You must tell us how you are getting on." Lady Compton was genuinely glad to see the young man. In some indescribable way, he made her feel closer to her son, lost to the ambitions of Napoléon.

The major, who had been her John's comrade, was a link to her fallen son. There was no real explaining it, but there was a comfort in seeing Major Tyndall. Perhaps it was no more than his being a gentleman of about the same age who had known John.

Gratified as Tyndall was to see the ladies out of deep mourning, he noted that sadness still lingered in their voices even though they greeted him with enthusiasm. He suspected it was a sorrow that would last a lifetime.

He was especially glad to see Lady Jane in a much improved state. She smiled at him shyly and a telltale blush covered her cheeks. At first Tyndall

146

was surprised by the charm directed toward him, but he returned the smile because he liked it.

"Mrs. Anseley has returned to London to begin the preparations for presenting my sister this Season. I am indebted to her, for the preparations are more complicated than a military campaign." Tyndall spoke with humor and a gratitude to Mrs. Anseley that was not lost on the ladies.

"I shall call upon Mrs. Anseley. I could have a party to honor your sister. Indeed, it is the very thing. We have been closed in this dark house with our grief too long. John would scoff at the idea of grieving for months," Lady Compton said, and her voice trembled with tears.

Tyndall knew the activity of planning a party would probably be good for them both.

"It would be grand to dance again," Lady Jane said with a wistful note to her voice.

Major Tyndall looked at Jane and recognized again just how charming a young lady she was. He smiled, and she dropped her eyes. She seemed so vulnerable. A gentle lady who needed someone to care for and protect her. She was no independent lady like Claire. Tyndall could not decide if that was a virtue or a fault. Perhaps it was a bit of both.

"Lady Jane, do you attend Lady Smather's ball?"

"Yes, Major, and I must admit I look forward to the evening."

Major Tyndall turned to Lady Compton. "May I escort you both? I am taking Eileen, and she will be delighted to be in Lady Jane's company. She needs to meet young people. It would give me great pleasure to do so." He received an ebullient reply, which he considered to be flattering to him and caused him to sit a little taller.

"Lady Compton, I will be grateful to have you call upon Mrs. Anseley. It is kind of you to suggest it. Her acquaintances are few. Having lived all her life in Yorkshire, she is just now making her way."

"Then it shall be done. I can only suppose she is someone I should like excessively, for you put such a high store on her."

"She has been very kind to us."

"Then perhaps I could be of assistance in getting your sister vouchers for Almack's. They are essential, you know."

"That would be most welcome. I do not know if I could secure them myself. This is all a bit overwhelming for a mere male." Tyndall chuckled.

"Then it is settled. I know the patronesses well."

"Eileen will be very pleased."

"Major Tyndall. Do tell me what Mrs. Anseley's husband's name was. I am curious."

"Richard . . . Richard Anseley." His heart skipped a beat, and little beads of perspiration appeared on his forehead. He feared what words were to come next. His fear materialized.

"How lovely. She must be related to the Earl of Wentworth. A fine gentleman and an Anseley, you know. Seek him out, if you have not. He will be pleased to help you." Lady Compton spoke with the assurance that she had imparted very helpful information.

Nathaniel looked surprised. "The Earl of Wentworth?"

"Yes, a true gentleman. A bit too dashing, perhaps, but a man of the highest order. He is a widower, you know, and has the dearest little girl. Pity she is motherless." Lady Compton sighed at the injustice of life.

Tyndall was at a loss for words. My God, what had he done?

"Julian Kent?"

"Julian Anseley Kent. Had to take the name of Kent in order to receive the honors of the earldom. The title comes from a very distant connection."

Nathaniel forced a smile. "Yes, I shall do that."

Their conversation turned back to Lady Smather's ball. Lady Jane's eyes shone with delight. Nathaniel was glad he had offered to escort them, but now he could hardly wait to take his leave.

The arrival of other callers gave Nathaniel an opportunity to escape. A time was set for his coming to escort them, and a promise was made by Lady Compton to call upon Mrs. Anseley within the next few days.

Nathaniel left the Comptons in total confusion. He had been so sure. Richard had spoken only of his uncle, who had bought him his colors. Surely a man would mention he was related to an earl? If this was true, why had he not heard it elsewhere?

My God, what a mess I have made, he thought. What could he do? That blackguard! Wentworth has known this all along and has given no indication. What is his game? The manner in which Wentworth looked at Claire was all the answer he needed. The knave earl looked like a bird of prey about to pounce on a mouse. Claire was certainly no mouse, but she did not know of Wentworth's deception! How could he tell her? He must, of course.

Would Wentworth expose her? Mayhap he *thinks* she is Richard's widow. Yes, that's it. No, for surely he would have mentioned his connection to Richard. The man is playing a deeper game. But what?

All his protective instincts leaped to the fore. He was fond of Claire. He could ask her to marry him and take her out of harm's way. What could he offer her? Nothing! Nathaniel's head started to pound. Protection. He must offer her protection. She would need it if the earl exposed her, or worse yet, used it for some nefarious design to get Claire in his arms. Eileen had been correct in seeing the look in the earl's eyes when he gazed upon Claire.

Perhaps he had time. The earl had not acted yet. He could only hope Wentworth was an honorable man and would not jeopardize Claire. *If* Wentworth even knew the situation: there was always the slim possibility he did not.

Nathaniel headed to his living quarters. His head was throbbing, and he needed to rest. Eventually he must tell Claire, but he could not bear to do so before the ball. Claire was looking forward to Lady Smather's ball. It was the first of the Season, and Wentworth had secured the invitations and was to be her escort.

Eileen had talked of nothing but the ball. He could not bear to spoil it all for them. After the ball he must tell Claire. He did not think the earl would do anything yet. Why he thought that, he could not answer. The earl had not done so yet and would not do so now, for whatever reason.

Major Tyndall entered the library early the next morning. He looked very handsome, despite the wee shadows that marked his fine eyes. Claire greeted him with a wide smile.

"Are you feeling all the thing, cousin?" she asked.

"Aye, but Claire, I must have words with you."

"My, my, you do sound serious. How can you be serious? Tonight is my first ball. I have the most beautiful gown in the realm. Oh, I tell you I am so happy." She seemed to shine.

Tyndall's heart began to pound. "Claire, do not make this any more difficult for me than necessary!"

"Difficult? What are you talking about? You sound far too serious." She laughed. "Come, sit here next to me, and I shall be the best of listeners."

Nathaniel took a deep breath and crossed the room to sit at her side. He rubbed his hands in a nervous gesture.

"Claire, hear me out. I come to ask for your hand in marriage. I have for some time been committed to you and your welfare. I have little to offer, but I could offer you protection, and I think we could make a happy family." He said the words hastily, as if they had been rehearsed.

Claire did not doubt for a moment that they had.

Still, his words rang with all the sincerity of his heart. Somehow she was surprised, yet in another way she was not. She remembered the hint she had received last year in Bath. She had been afraid this might happen. In all ways she had treated him as a favored brother. The timing surprised her.

She knew she had depended on him too much in the early days, and perhaps now he could see she needed him less. Was that why he now spoke?

"Nate, you need not be told how I feel about you. I love you. I love you as a brother, a mentor, but—"

"Not as an object of affection," he said with a slight derisive sound.

"Always affection. Not as a lover. Nate, I have no intention of marrying—ever. This Season will be my one adventure in the glitter of society. I shall return to the country. It is what I know best. I may travel the world, but with my inheritance I can take care of Phoebe and myself."

"Claire, you should marry. You should have children. I could make you happy. I know it."

"Yes, probably more so than anyone I know, but—"

"It is the Earl of Wentworth, isn't it."

A deadly silence fell in the room. Claire flushed and began to tremble. It was the truth. Nathaniel had seen the truth before she had.

"He is not for you, Claire. He is dangerous."

"I know. He would not be an easy man to live with. I fear he is far too opinionated and unlikely to compromise."

"You have apparently given it much thought."

"I have my conclusion—he is far too much for me to handle."

Tyndall gave a laugh. "You may have to. I have found out he is Richard's uncle." He had not intended to raise the subject until after the ball, but it would have been dishonest to keep such information from her. After all, she was to be in the earl's company this evening, and she should be forewarned.

Claire gasped. "So that is it! That is why you rush to press marriage on me—to protect me! And I knew there was something about him. The intensity of his looks. I thought perhaps he was taken with . . . but, no . . . he is wondering if I am who I say I am."

"He may or may not know," Tyndall offered.

"Aye, that may be. I will not force his hand. Let us see what the Earl of Wentworth has in mind." She narrowed her eyes as if she now saw a clearer meaning to his actions.

"Claire, my offer is sincere. It may have been precipitated by the earl, but I am truly afraid for you. The scandal would ruin you."

"Oh, Nate, I understand. I know your offer to be a noble one. You cannot sacrifice yourself to protect me. We are bound in friendship."

Tyndall leaned over and placed a kiss on her cheek. "Some couples do not have even that. Claire, I am always here. You gave me a reason to live. Survive, I did. Let us speak no more of this now. There is time to see what is yet to come."

"I knew I could depend on you, Nate. I am ever grateful for all you have done."

He rose to take his leave. "I am here, remember that. The Earl of Wentworth can deal you no harm."

Claire wondered if the harm had already been done. She had lost her heart to a man who was playing a false game, if he did indeed know she had not married his nephew. But she could not censure him, for she was playing a false game herself, with less acceptable reason.

Nathaniel reached the door and turned around. "Claire, we did have some fun."

"Aye, Nate. The chance of a lifetime. It has been wonderful. We'll see Eileen through the Season and bid farewell to a dream."

Seventeen

Claire sat staring into space. So, our dashing Earl of Wentworth was playing at a game of deception just as she was. What could be his purpose? Her motive had started out innocent enough—merely to escape her dreary life and reach out to some fun and excitement.

However, she thought, a lie is never innocent. She had meant to involve no one but herself, and surely it could not really harm anyone. She smiled derisively, wondering how many men faced the gallows with just such a declaration. Could her counterfeit widowhood harm anyone?

It had seemed such a good idea to lend credibility to her tale by making her deceased husband real. That had been a fatal flaw. Now she wished she had made up some fictitious name. John Smith would have done. With her luck they would have met someone of the same regiment. That someone would have declared loud and clear (in the presence of the archbishop of Canterbury, no less) that no such personage ever served in such and such a regiment.

She shrugged. In any case she would have had to name a regiment. She sighed. Lies begot lies.

Claire rose and stepped through the French doors into the garden. The weather was as beautiful as she could remember. She thought of the silver-and-cream dress waiting for this evening's ball.

What was her next move? Should she continue her deception or explain it all to Wentworth? Oh, how *that* thought rankled! She could just see his superior stare down his aristocratic nose! No, she could not humble herself to say she was a liar. Claire cringed at the word. She had never put her escapade in just that strong a term. She blushed.

Would he suspect her to be a gold digger? No, he could not, for she would have declared her connection to the earl as a means of seeking some advantage. Wentworth had sought *her* out! All moves had been precipitated by him! Then why had he not said a word? He was not sure of her true status, that was why.

Well, she thought, she could not turn back the clock. The die was cast. She would appear this evening on the arm of the arrogant earl and flourish the most dazzling of smiles.

If he wondered at her marriage, let him prove she was not married to his relative. Her first impulse was to run, but she would not. She would stand her ground—lie and all. As soon as Eileen had her come-out ball, Claire could retreat from the scene and go home to Rosehill.

She was not ready to return to country life. It was inevitable that she would eventually, but not now. If only the terrible war were over, they could ravel the continent. See the world. The war went on and on. Someday it would end and she would ravel then.

Tonight was the problem at hand. She would go and see a glittering ballroom and hopefully dance every dance. It had been a dream all her growing years, and the Earl of Wentworth could continue whatever scheme he was engaged in, since she had chosen to do the same.

"You will be enchanted with the palace, and especially the magnificent ballroom. It is unique in all of London. Perhaps the only true Rococo house in all England," the Earl of Wentworth explained to Phoebe and Claire after they were comfortably seated and underway.

"It was built by Baroness Von Slagelhauen about sixty years ago. She was the mistress of a minor Bavarian prince and apparently came away from the liaison a very wealthy woman. When the prince married for political reasons, she was banished from the principality by the new wife, apparently at a considerable price. At any rate, you will see a magnificent villa that belongs on the Danube. When you enter the ballroom, you will think you have been transported to Austria. It is magnificent."

"I have heard of the baroness's villa. How did the Smathers come by it?" Phoebe asked.

"The baroness decreed in her will that it could be sold only if the buyer signed an agreement that no change be made to the interiors. When you see it, you will know that it would be a crime to change any aspect of the interiors. In a day of classical revival it is a refreshing sight. Odd, how the old can seem new." He chuckled.

"It is a shame that is not so with old people," Phoebe said with a sly twinkle.

"Oh, I quite disagree with you. Some of the most refreshing people I know come from a previous generation. Nothing like a bit of experience to give one an interesting perspective. Do you agree, Mrs. Anseley?"

Claire wondered if there was a hidden meaning behind his words. But she was not going to spend the evening fretting over whether he meant this or that. "I most certainly do. My aunt is years younger than I in wit and wisdom."

The earl smiled, and Claire decided he was far too good-looking for her own good. And she was sure he knew it. She lifted her chin and turned to gaze at the crush of carriages making their way to the entrance of Lord and Lady Smather's fine mansion.

"Who's the vision on Wentworth's arm?" Viscount Byrne asked while raising his quizzing glass with an elegant, languid motion. "I say, she is quite a beauty."

Wakeford turned in Byrne's indicated direction. "Indubitably. I must have an introduction. Count on Julian to find the fairest of the fair." He chuckled.

"Let's go and pounce on them. See if we can pry her away. Great sport. I shall enjoy his threatening scowl. Far too high-and-mighty by half," Lord Wakeford said.

His companion chuckled and agreed.

Claire gasped at the magnificence of the ballroom they had just entered. "I never saw or even dreamed of such a room. It is a palace!" The awe in her voice was unmistakable.

"I never cease to marvel at the sparkle of candlelight reflecting in the mirrors. It is dazzling. Lifts the spirits.

"It is like entering one's imagination. And it would have to be a vivid imagination, for I could never have dreamed up such magnificence. If I could have chosen a ballroom for my first ball, it would indeed have been this one." She raised her eyes to the towering earl and fluttered them.

The sincerity of her voice was not lost on him even though she struck humor into it. He smiled, delighted to see her so happy.

"Are you flirting with me, Mrs. Anseley?"

Claire snapped open her fan. "Now that is just like a man—so sure that every lady is taken by his highly overrated charms." She sent him a dazzling smile.

"Gammon, pure gammon!"

"Your lordship, I am just a country girl, lately come to town. I know of no such behavior." She smiled sweetly.

A tiny frown flickered, then disappeared. "Surely your late husband was subject to your winning

159

wiles," Wentworth teased, but it was not all teasing. He felt his pulse quicken.

Watching her reaction, he noted her eyes widen slightly. Did he see pain in her expression? He saw something as she put her fan into motion. He regretted his chiding.

"Come, they are forming a set. I have waited forever to hold you in my arms."

"Now it is your turn for flirting!"

He laughed. "Perhaps, Mrs. Anseley. Then again perhaps I am utterly serious."

When they reached the dance floor, she took her place before him, secretly grateful for her recent dance lessons.

"You are thoroughly pretty, Mrs. Anseley."

"Shush." Claire raised her hand in caution. " 'Tis not seemly. You are too unkind to put me to the blush. What if someone heard?"

"Heard me tell a lady she was pretty? You are right; I should have said *beautiful*. Besides, my dear, they would think it far more odd if I did not. My compliments are legion." He smiled devilishly.

Somehow she did not believe he threw overdrawn compliments around. She tossed her curls, then smiled to herself. She was far too old to display such a girlish ploy. Ah, but little she cared. Tonight was her night!

She smiled in genuine appreciation and was rewarded by a heart-stopping smile of understanding. She would never understand the man, but he seemed to read her mind.

"Lord Wentworth, I never know how to take you."

"Simply take me. Question not, my dear Mrs. Anseley."

Claire laughed. Her eyes sparkled, and she was adorable, Wentworth thought. He wondered if he was getting in over his head. He watched the thrilling evening set her heart soaring as a light whisper of wind. Wentworth was content to let her shine. In fact, she fairly took his breath away.

When the dance ended, he guided her back to Phoebe. It would call too much attention if he took the next dance with her or stayed in her pocket. He would wait until later to seek her out, when it was less likely to be noticed. The name of Anseley was sure to come up.

Lords Byrne and Wakeford bore down upon the smiling couple.

"Wentworth, good to see you. How goes the struggle in Parliament? I heard you even gave a speech. What are things coming to? But first, my good man, introduce me to this divine creature."

"Mrs. Anseley, may I present the most notorious flirt in the realm, Lord Byrne. Mrs. Anseley, widowed by the war." He said this on purpose. He did not want the question of her name answered here.

"My condolences, Mrs. Anseley. Surely your husband was—"

Wentworth frowned and raised his hand to halt his speech. "Mrs. Anseley joins us this evening to dance for the first time since her bereavement. We shall not spoil it. Mrs. Anseley, I am correct, am I not?"

Claire flushed with a flitting look of sadness. Wentworth regretted mentioning her situation, but he had meant to forestall any questions. But she looked so stricken. Damn.

The two lords' heads bobbed up and down. "Agreed. Tonight is a night for light music and thought. Mrs. Anseley, may I have this dance?"

Claire dropped a curtsy and took his proffered arm.

The evening passed in a whirl of introductions. Names and faces all passed in a pace of confusion, too many for Claire to remember. Her happiness imparted a grace that enthralled those she met. The kindest compliments passed among the guests, and from the evening's success Claire achieved an outstanding introduction into London society. Her future was assured.

Sir Reginald Henton, whom she had met in Bath, exclaimed with delight when he espied her on the arm of an adoring gallant. "Mrs. Anseley, you naughty, naughty girl. You left Bath with nary a by-your-leave. I daresay, you broke my heart."

Claire smiled sweetly. "It is good to see you. I beg your pardon, but it was on a very imperative matter that I returned to London."

"You will redeem yourself by granting a dance."

"I shall be delighted." She took his arm and headed to the dance floor.

And so the evening passed in a whirl of dances and new faces.

Wentworth claimed her later for another dance.

"My lord, I am almost weary. I am afraid this is not meant for those above nineteen." She laughed.

"Then let us escape to the garden. It is unbearably hot in here."

They strolled out onto the terrace. The night was soft and warm and a welcome relief from the stuffy ballroom. Others strolled among the garden walks beside the sprinkling fountains.

Claire sighed. "I shall remember this night forever. It is so beautiful, almost enough to be painful."

Wentworth looked sharply to her. "There will be others."

"No, my lord. You see, I was trying to capture what I had missed. I now know that is not possible. One is a girl only once. I am no longer a girl. Still, it has been a most wonderful evening."

The soft shadows and pale moonlight played about her, giving her an ethereal light. Suddenly she seemed almost fey, as if she was slipping away. It was an odd premonition (if indeed it was that). As if he was being warned. Wentworth dismissed the uncomfortable feeling. It was too vague and opposite his usual solid thinking. She was here, all flesh and blood. He wanted to reach out and hold her so she would not escape.

The music could be heard as they wandered along the path. From time to time Wentworth acknowledged an acquaintance with a nod. They reached the end of the walk beside the shimmering, ornamental lake. The moon sent silvery lights that danced on the water. The beauty of it all erased the line between dream and reality.

Entering some shadows, Wentworth gently pulled Claire into his arms. She did not resist. The evening was too magical and the night too seductive and the man too irresistible. His lips were warm and his embrace was all and even more than any girlish dream could conjure.

She remained in his arms savoring the exhilaration of her emotions. He lifted her chin and kissed her again. But this time the kiss demanded more. He crossed a threshold that Claire had not yet reached or understood.

"My lord, please . . ." she said, and broke from his embrace. He was more than she had expected, and warning signals surfaced. "We must return, for surely we will be missed."

"Claire, I have thought of this moment a dozen times." He reached to draw her nearer.

"My Lord Wentworth, I declare, you make a girl lose her senses." She tried to sound lighthearted and flirty, but she felt neither. Her heart was behaving badly, and she longed to fling herself back into his arms.

"You are no girl, Mrs. Anseley. Do not turn away." There was a husky pleading to his voice.

She laughed a silly little nervous laugh. "My lord, we are not yet betrothed."

Not yet betrothed? The words staggered him. His fiery passion died instantly. Betrothed? My God, where did she get that idea? What had he said? Surely a kiss . . .

"Forgive me. Please forgive my unwelcome ardor." He took her arm, and they slowly retraced their steps without speaking for several minutes.

"Make allowances for the romantic night. Not like any I have seen. You will forgive me?"

Claire glanced at him, but the shadowy night did not reveal his expression. "It is forgotten," she replied primly.

"That puts me in my place. Forgotten! I shall not likely do so," he said in a low whisper. He could not quite understand her. There was an air of innocence, the ingenue, and yet she was a woman, a widow, with a warm response to his first kiss. There were passion and fire in her. Perhaps it was too soon after her husband's death. He would have to tread more carefully.

They walked on, but the magic had now vanished as the chill in the air spread across the garden and into their bodies.

Eighteen

The hum of voices and laughter drifted into the foyer as Wentworth handed the butler his hat, gloves, and walking stick. He was ushered into the salon to find a veritable crush of callers. Claire stood in the middle of half-a-dozen foolish swains, batting her eyes at their silly sallies. My God, the chit is a hit, Wentworth thought. He frowned.

His earlier idea of capturing her first faded. She obviously had her pick of admirers. He could hardly credit that she would be in the marriage market again, but after her remark last evening he was not sure. Why anyone would want to marry a second time, he could not fathom. She was obviously having a grand time in the middle of the foolish grins and drooling compliments.

"Morning, Miss Greene," he said to Phoebe, who had come to greet him.

"Nice to see you, Wentworth. Last evening's ball was lovely. Thank you for escorting us. Claire has sent you an invitation to Eileen's come-out. We are counting on you."

"I am not sure how long I shall be in London."

"You must remain long enough to attend Eileen's come-out ball. We quite depend on you. By the by, you are invited to a small gathering next Friday, but I shall leave that to Claire to issue." Smiling in genuine friendship, she seemed to command his acceptance.

He nodded. "Thank you, Miss Greene. I shall—"

Claire's soft voice interrupted, and he turned to her approach. "Lord Wentworth, I am so glad you have called. Thank you again for your escort, and for the lovely flowers you sent. You are too kind."

He sent her a wary, tentative smile. Kindness was not his motive. His eyes scanned the many floral tributes that graced the room.

"I challenge you to remember my humble offering."

"Yellow roses on the piano, my lord."

He arched an eyebrow. "I am flattered, indeed. I have never seen the likes of your success. A beautiful widow is hardly unheard of but seldom lights a bonfire."

Their eyes met and held. She wondered whether she read a hint of censure or humor.

"Perhaps my fortune has come to the attention of many. I will not deny my delight in my success, as you call it, but then it does not change anything, does it?" She knew her words to be a trifle sharp, but he had annoyed her. She turned from him to bid farewell to several departing guests.

He waited for the crush to thin before he approached her again. "Miss Greene has extended a dinner invitation for Friday evening. I look forward to seeing you then." His words held a caressing edge. He bowed and departed.

As she watched him leave, a vague, uneasy feeling engulfed her. She must be wary of him, and it was not just the name of Anseley that worried her.

Claire glanced at Phoebe, who nodded slightly, as if to indicate that all went well. Knowing her dinner party had been a success, Claire beamed back. She would face Eileen's come-out with more confidence. She was finding her ability to organize a party as efficiently as she ran a house. The austere training under Simon's eagle eye had produced an unexpected dividend. Compared to thinking of every possibility concerning every penny spent, it was a mere trifle remembering only what needed to be done.

She surveyed her guests. The gentlemen had joined the ladies after their port. Everyone looked happy and satisfied. Mrs. Harper had outdone herself. The salmon with dill sauce had been perfection. Everything had been delicious. The conversation had been lively and entertaining.

She noticed Nate engaged in a conversation with Lady Jane, who seemed to hang on his every word. The young lady was besotted. Good, Nate needed someone to lean on him.

Her gaze went to Wentworth, who stood by the mantel looking annoyingly marvelous—as always. She lifted her chin. Having only herself to thank for having had little opportunity to speak with him this evening, she frowned. She had not placed him next to herself on purpose and now rather regretted it. Should she cross over and talk to him? She toyed with the ribbons on her dress.

"At last, I find you!"

Claire started and turned in horror as the sound of a loud, booming voice filled the air, bringing all conversation to a halt. Squire Bradley entered, wearing dusty traveling clothes, and strode into the parlor like Grete raking hell. Perkins was close behind, flapping his arms about and looking aghast. He shot Claire a helpless, apologetic look.

In the calmest voice she could muster, Claire asked, "Squire Bradley, what brings you to London, and to my home, at this time of night?"

Bradley espied Wentworth. "Aha, you! I should have known." He turned to Claire. "You had no right to leave without informing me. We are to be married, have you forgotten?"

Claire gasped and stepped back. "Squire Bradley, I ask you to leave this minute. This is not the time or the place to discuss this." Her legs were trembling.

"I don't trust you won't go flying off as before. You are obliged to marry me. We are promised."

The guests sat or stood rooted. They stared in shocked silence.

"Never," Claire snapped, tears beginning to surface.

Bradley raised his hand and pointed to Claire. "She ain't married neither. Never was." He wagged his finger. "You are not Mrs. Anseley."

The rich, resonant voice of the earl cut through the confusing and shocking scene. "Squire Bradley, you are mistaken. She was married to my nephew and sadly widowed soon after the wedding. She is under my protection." He moved deliberately toward Bradley in a slow, menacing manner.

Everyone stared in disbelief as the scene unfolded before them. All happened so fast, it was seconds before the guests could grasp the meaning of this outrageous intrusion.

Major Tyndall struggled to his feet at the sight of Claire's white face and wide eyes. He moved toward the raging squire just as Wentworth crossed the room. Phoebe was almost faint, and the others just stared.

"She ain't married. I say she ain't. She's a fraud."

Wentworth grabbed Bradley's arm and began to force him from the room. "I think it wise you leave. You are offending the widow of my nephew, and for that I call you out. Have your seconds call on me. I shall have my satisfaction for this insult."

Bradley shoved Wentworth and moved to grab Claire's arm. "You ain't getting away this time." His eyes were wild, and his breath smelled of whiskey. He was angry and drunk.

Claire fainted. It was the only thing she could think of to do.

Wentworth, who had moved to separate the squire from Claire, was there to catch her fall. He scooped her up into his arms.

Phoebe was on her feet. "This way." And she

urried from the room with Wentworth following. Ie held Claire tightly.

Claire's eyelids fluttered.

"Keep them closed," the earl whispered as he :limbed the steps behind Aunt Phoebe. He smiled with pleasure when Will and Jamie rushed past ıim into the parlor. That would be the end of Bradey for the evening, and tomorrow he would kill ıim.

Tyndall cursed his infirmities, his helplessness, ıntil he realized he had his arm around softly weeping Lady Jane. The poor dear, she needed his protection. "There, there, it's nothing to cry over. Everything's going to be fine. I am here to take care of you. The man is obviously mad."

His feeling of helplessness vanished. He was providing a protective arm for Lady Jane, while the Dalton boys roughly ushered Bradley out. Tyndall smiled faintly. He had not been able to enter the fray, but he could offer comfort.

A babble arose from the guests, with each speaking at once and exclaiming that one wasn't safe even in one's own home. What was this world coming to?

Meanwhile the earl gently laid Claire on her bed while Phoebe and Dora scampered about finding smelling salts and a cold compress.

"It is safe now," he softly whispered.

Claire's eyes flew open.

He stood smiling. "Ah, the fair widow Anseley's web has captured not only the hearts of London but also half the realm, it seems. Sleep well, Mrs. An seley; your party was a success and diverting. I shall call in the morning. After all, you are now under my protection!"

"You won't duel with Bradley, will you? Promise you won't!"

"Do I detect some concern on your behalf? I am flattered. I had not realized I had come up so in your estimation. Fear not, I am a renowned shot."

"He is, too!" she whispered.

"Would you care if I died for your honor?"

She turned away, with tears now trailing down her cheeks. "Please, just don't duel with him."

"I have called him out. My honor is at stake—yours, too!"

She placed her hand on his sleeve. His other hand covered hers.

"My honor is not worth it," she whispered.

Phoebe and Dora reentered the room just in time to see him bend down and kiss Claire's forehead. They stood astounded.

"That is for me to decide, dearest relative. Fear not. I shall not die. If I thought those tears were for me, it might be worth it."

"Beast!" she hissed.

"Aha, she is fine, back to her feisty self. No harm done," he said to the ladies, who stood with gaping mouths.

With a slight bow and a dazzling smile he took his leave. "I shall call tomorrow morning to see how you are getting on."

* * *

His lordship did call the next morning as promised, looking very fit, indeed. He walked with a buoyant step and an expectant expression.

Standing at the window overlooking Claire's garden, he waited with his shoulders squared, his feet slightly apart, and his hands behind his back. He appeared totally relaxed. Yet there was an underlying tension, an alertness, as he turned at Claire's entrance.

Dressed in a soft yellow morning dress, she looked as charming as spring sunshine. She entered with a heightened color and a lift to her chin. She was all that is feminine, yet she carried a sense of herself.

"Good morning, my Lord Wentworth," she said simply as she crossed the room to stand before him.

He looked expectantly for her aunt to come into the room, but she did not.

"I am surprised to see you so early. My aunt has not even arisen. The evening's events just about did her in."

"I am not surprised. It was very unfortunate. But I thought perhaps you were worried lest I had perished on the field of honor." His eyes twinkled.

"I see you are safe from harm's way. And Squire Bradley?"

"Squire Bradley has taken care of Squire Bradley," he said.

"How so?"

"He left London last night with the satisfaction of having distressed you as revenge for spurning

173

his offers. His safety is assured and his honor in shreds, for he chose not to meet the challenge." The earl's eyes still held the hint of amusement.

Claire was not sure if he was amused by the situation of last evening, by Bradley, or by her predicament. She studied him a moment. He returned her gaze evenly. Neither spoke. The silence was not in anticipation of what was to be said next, but an exchange of mutual involvement in a very awkward situation.

"My reputation will be on the tongue of every tabby for days." She sighed.

"Probably. Or until another seven-day wonder arises. The ton has a very short memory. Besides, I stand your champion. Few will challenge my word on the matter of your marriage. Bradley will be passed off as some mad, rejected suitor. Might even add to your stature." He laughed.

"It is not one tiny bit funny."

"The world is ever ready to forgive a charming lady and can hardly fault her because her admirers cannot take no for an answer." He acted as though it were not too serious a problem.

He is entertained by all this, Claire realized. The idea both annoyed and pleased her. She would be fortunate to get away with merely "amusing" his lordship when he found out about her masquerade as his nephew's widow. How was she to know her unfortunate choice of a "husband" would land on his family tree? She smiled a little, too. If it were not so horrifying, it would be amusing.

"May I ring for tea?" she asked.

"No, but you could answer a question for me."

"Sit down, please. Of course. What would you like to know?"

"I would like to know about you and Richard."

Nineteen

"I suppose I should begin at the beginning," Claire said.

"A wise choice." His jade eyes penetrated hers.

She shifted uncomfortably. "Do be seated."

"I prefer to stand." He placed his arms across his chest and waited.

Claire stepped back. He was too disconcerting, and telling him was not going to be easy. She dropped her eyes.

In that instant Wentworth knew the truth: she was *not* Richard's widow! His weeks of speculation evaporated. For some strange reason he felt relieved. Why, he could not explain. He waited.

"My lord, I am nine and twenty," she said.

"You look a decade younger. Your life must have been without sorrow—except for Richard, of course."

She shot him a quelling look. "If you want my answer, you are going to have to listen."

He showed his even white teeth in a devilish smile. "My apologies; I am all attention."

"You're mocking me!"

"Mocking you? I am waiting with bated breath to hear of your marriage and sad widowhood."

She turned and began to pace. "Not to win your sympathy, but life has not been easy under the demanding dictates of a martinet stepfather. Upon his death I learned I was a woman of considerable means. This fact had been kept from me, for God only knows what reason. My mother's bequest had grown for twenty years untouched while we lived in increasing poverty. Simon had about depleted Rosehill and its treasures. He could not sell the land or house, for they are mine."

"I am gratified to know you will not lack for the next meal, but what has all this to do with Richard?"

"Hush. Listen. When I discovered I was a lady of means, you can imagine my joy. I could now take care of Phoebe, buy pretty clothes, refurbish Rosehill, whatever I wished." She stopped and looked at him for any sign of understanding.

"The lure of London sights and the joy of society beckoned. You see, I never made a come-out. Never left Rosehill. Never danced the night away."

Her voice became soft and carried a wistful longing not lost on the sentiments of his lordship. His hand rose involuntarily to reach out and touch her, then dropped. He wished he could withdraw from the conversation.

What began as a desire to be in her presence in the highly charged atmosphere of the "chase" had suddenly turned, and the power of his emotions toward her threatened to engulf him.

"Mrs. Anseley, I need hear no more. You need not explain yourself to me. I apologize. I really did not mean to intrude."

Claire turned and met his eyes. The apology stabbed her. She felt even more deceitful. "You do not yet understand. I owe you as much, 'uncle.'" She offered a wan smile.

"Phoebe tried to discourage me when I seized upon the plan to play the 'widow,'" she continued. "I am far too old and too long on the shelf. A widow is more interesting than an ape leader."

"And allowed you more freedom and respect," he interjected.

"Exactly. So I chose to pose as a widow—a rich one." She smiled, and the elusive dimple appeared. "How Richard?"

"I enlisted Major Tyndall, and we felt a real person would lend more credibility."

"I agree. Were you Mrs. Anseley when you commandeered my room at the Royal Rose?"

"No, I was still Miss Darington. I had not yet met Major Tyndall or his sister. We just did not anticipate Squire Bradley's persistence or your arrival on the scene. We did not know you even existed."

"While I fault Squire Bradley's method of courtship, I can understand his persistence."

Claire was positive a glint of humor had again entered his eyes. "I assure you it is the charm of my land, not me, that ensures his devotion!" she said, and she lifted her chin as fire lit her eyes.

"My dear Mrs. Anseley, I must disagree with you.

While I am sure your land holdings are allurement enough for Bradley, you will not fault me for pointing out that you are adorable and totally irresistible."

He reached out. She stepped back.

"Your lordship need not put pretty words on deceit. I apologize for all this. I did so want to present Miss Tyndall and enjoy a Season."

"What is to prevent you from doing so?"

Her eyes widened. "I have been exposed!"

"By a lovesick country bumpkin who was unaware of your marriage to my nephew."

"You would do that for me?" she whispered.

"I would slay dragons for you. Of course you may be Mrs. Anseley. A decided addition to our beleaguered family tree." He chuckled.

"What of your family?"

"Alas, there is only me to object, and I do not."

"Why would you do this for me?" she asked with relief flooding her. She was safe from censure! He would protect her name.

When he stepped forward this time, she stood transfixed by his smoldering eyes and the relief his words brought.

Slipping his arms around her waist, he drew her lightly to him. His kiss was first light and teasing. His arms were strong, and she felt safe. He would keep her secret, and she returned his kiss in a rush of gratitude.

He held her close against his lean body. His kisses demanded more, and a heady fire swept through them both. There was no denying the sexual attraction.

"My adorable, adorable widow. I have thought of nothing else for days. You have haunted me night and day. Say you will be mine."

"Oh, yes, Wentworth. I cannot refuse you. You have been in my thoughts far too often." She pulled away. "We will have to postpone our announcement. I cannot seem to rush into marriage so soon after your nephew's death."

Marriage. He stepped back and dropped his hands. How clumsy he had been to make his offer in words she did not understand! It was born in the beginning of their acquaintance, when he knew her as a widow who might be lonely and agreeable to an *affaire d'amour.*

"You look thunderstruck, my lord."

"I am. I had not thought to wed again and considered you a widow. . . ."

"And therefore just anxious for your attentions! How conceited you are."

"You cannot deny our attraction to one another. I am offering love for love alone."

Her eyes widened. "How ironic. Squire Bradley offers marriage for my land. You offer your protection for my bed. Why do you suppose I feel there is no bargain in either?" She scoffed. "I decline."

"Claire, I was clumsy. I mean no insult. I truly believe we might spend a wonderful time together."

"And when passion dies, we go our separate ways?"

"It is better than being trapped in an unhappy marriage. I know; I have done so."

"I may be a spinster and a green girl, but some-how I thought love transcended all that. Well, love is not just passion, is it? And passion not love."

"Claire, I thought I was offering love."

"Not to last a lifetime."

"Love does not last. It is an illusion. We must take what is offered, for it is all too fleeting."

"Not *my* love, your lordship. Good day to you. I categorically decline. You would come away from the affair unscathed, and I would be a whore."

Claire walked to the door and opened it. She stood aside for him to pass through.

He paused in front of her. "Claire, I do love you. We may never, ever have such a chance again."

"You egotistical dolt! I have an offer for love and marriage."

"Tyndall?"

"Aye. He is honorable."

Wentworth shut the door and pulled her into his arms. He kissed her very thoroughly. "Now, can Tyndall offer that?"

Claire slapped him. "No, my lord, he cannot. But it is not enough. This may come as a shock to your arrogant eminence, but your offer is simply not enough!"

Julian Anseley Kent was both arrogant and spoiled, but he was not without understanding. Since the death of his wife some six years before, he had not once considered marriage. He had not met anyone who gave him even a passing thought to do so. He regretted his insulting offer.

He had allowed his unpardonable passion to cloud his mind and actions. How could he have been so stupid? He was appalled at his conduct, and yet he had acted with premeditated steps.

The fact that she was not a widow and was in probability a virgin had not entered his thoughts. He had treated her like a woman of easy virtue, one who would succumb to his passionate embrace. Such behavior was simply not acceptable in this day and age, and he had violated every prescribed requirement of a gentleman.

He was crushed by his crass behavior, appalled by it. How could he have so miscalculated the scene? His passion and desire had gone ahead of reason, and he had played the fool to his emotions. The insult to Claire brought him near despair.

How could he have allowed those gold-brown eyes and that winsome smile to bring him to a quivering mass of stupidity? He could not berate himself enough. A bottle of brandy, a night of remorse, and a quaking head that kept him in bed offered no release from his self-flagellation.

When he at last rose from his bed the following afternoon (his head still throbbing), he managed to pen a letter:

My dear Mrs. Anseley,

I can offer no excuse for my topic of conversation other than to say that I beg your forgiveness. Could you possibly see your way to allow me a short visit? Pen and paper do not allow me the freedom to speak freely for fear the letter may be intercepted.

May I please call to express my sorrow?

JK

The Earl of Wentworth

At first Claire had been outraged by the insufferable, arrogant, and presumptuous earl. How dare he insult her, was her first response. Still, he had not offered the least censure of her deception and lying about being the widow of his relative. How justified he would have been to condemn her outright. Yet he had listened to her reasons, seeing humor in them and accepting her explanation. Was she to offer him less? How was she to sit in judgment when she had bent the truth to serve herself? He, at least, had been forthright. He had said he was enamored—even went as far as saying he loved her and desired her as his mistress. At least he had been honest by offering no artful seduction.

She blushed at the thought of her response to his searing kisses and didn't doubt for one moment that under the right setting she may very well have ended up in his bed. She had to, in all honesty, thank him for that, since she found him exceedingly irresistible. An offer of marriage would have been accepted in a minute.

The fact that he did not offer marriage cut to the quick. Still, he had stood by her and salvaged her reputation. She must consent to see him. She owed him that much. If he could forgive her, she must do no less.

She sent him a written reply that she would see him the next day at ten o'clock.

She rose at his entrance at precisely ten o'clock. He was even more appealing than before because his glance was at once soft and held his entreaty.

He bowed over her hand. "You are too kind. I appreciate the opportunity to tell you of my sorrow and beg your forgiveness."

"It is done. You are forgiven."

"My offer was misguided but genuine. I now ask that you allow me to further your place in society. The place you seek and want."

Claire blushed. It sounded so . . . contriving, so opportunistic on her part.

"I vow I shall never cross the bounds of propriety. Have no fear that I would again mistake my desire for yours. It will give me a great deal of pleasure to escort you until it is time to return to Dublin."

"How can you accept my deception? Does it not rankle you that I play Richard's widow?"

"Claire . . . May I call you Claire? I wish we had met under different circumstances, but neither of us can change what is past. The dead are beyond us, and only the living can make amends. Richard cares not what we do. You said you intended to leave London after this Season. I have no doubt you will marry. In a year or two Richard's widow will be forgotten."

He is right, she thought. She would pass from the scene, leaving no permanent mark. She would become only a vague memory, then be forgotten.

"I accept. Until Eileen's come-out, a truce. We will be friends."

"Always that, Mrs. Anseley, always that. I am ever at your service." He nodded and took his leave.

Her heart hammered in her chest and temples. If only he could have offered more or she accepted less.

Twenty

Claire and Phoebe were gratified by events following Bradley's dreadful disclosure. At least Claire and Phoebe no longer had the worry of being exposed as frauds, thanks to the Earl of Wentworth's rescue. Both breathed a sigh of relief, especially Claire.

Lady Compton called shortly after Wentworth's visit to offer her aid, declaring she had secured vouchers for Eileen to attend Almack's and insisting on escorting her along with Lady Jane next Wednesday evening. Claire readily agreed, as Almack's was a must for any young lady entering the marriage mart. It was not Claire's wish to join them. She would leave that to others.

Next Lady Compton begged Claire to allow her to cosponsor Eileen. She wished to join forces for her come-out ball and by that, show her solid support. It would be the best way to stifle the tabby tongues, she insisted. Claire agreed, for Lady Compton was a stickler of the highest order, and her sponsorship was almost an assurance of success.

Callers continued to arrive, some out of curiosity, others in sympathy. Some questioned the incident, and others, while not mentioning the unfortunate affair, also lent their support. The whole disclosure seemed to pass as unfounded and the work of an unstable, rejected suitor. It seemed to give the dashing widow a bit of stature. After all, Mrs. Anseley was exceedingly attractive, some pointed out. Little damage seemed to have occurred because of the vengeful squire.

As the days rolled by, Wentworth continued to call and escorted them on two carriage rides through the park. This reinforced his endorsement of the authenticity of his nephew's widow. What better proof?

If Claire's proximity bothered the earl, it was not discernible. He was all that is proper and polite. The solicitous relative—no more than that.

Claire seldom found his eyes upon her. He treated her with kindly detachment, as he would treat any friend. How she behaved, she was not sure, for he invariably left her breathless. His nearness sent her heart racing. If he accidentally brushed her arm or held her hand a second too long, her breath disappeared.

She wondered at her foolishness. She had made her choice, and that was that. Finally she came to accept that she was in love with the earl—desperately and irrevocably in love. The pain was almost unbearable. She began to wonder if she should have accepted his carte blanche and seized the chance for love, however fleeting.

She shook her head at these thoughts. No matter how painful it was now, it would have been more so if he had grown tired of her. He had said as much. She believed him.

Therefore, she stiffened her resolve to the task of remaining her usual self. She wanted no one to know her heart and the source of her pain, least of all Aunt Phoebe. She would see Eileen launched, stay a short while, then leave London before summer set in. For now she hid these thoughts and made every effort to appear as ordinary as possible. How successful she was, she was not sure and she could not ask.

Phoebe, of course, knew something was amiss. Since she had no knowledge of Wentworth's scandalous offer or subsequent visit, she thought Claire's dissatisfaction lay in the ever-increasing attention by Major Tyndall to Lady Jane Compton. Phoebe carefully avoided calling attention to that obviously growing affection.

As the days passed, Phoebe grew more mystified, since Claire always met Tyndall and Lady Jane with the greatest delight and even accompanied them on excursions. The sadness in Claire's eyes, Phoebe surmised, did not come from the major's defection.

She realized this the night of Eileen's ball. The Earl of Wentworth bowed over Claire's hand during the reception at the beginning of the ball and during his farewell at his departure. He had not danced with Claire, not even once. She remembered his words at his departure.

"Eileen's ball is a resounding success, my dear Mrs. Anseley. You are to be commended. In fact, you are a success. The darling of the fickle ton."

Phoebe watched his smile, a smile that would leave even an old lady weak-kneed. She heard Claire catch her breath. She saw Claire's rising color and trembling lips.

"Thank you, my lord. It is an evening to remember in more ways than one," Claire said.

"Then I leave you in good hands," he said. Then he smiled at Phoebe, and she saw pain in his eyes.

"You are returning to Dublin?" Claire asked.

"Yes, soon. So I take leave of you now. I shall think of you often. Take care of yourself and find a good, solid husband." He turned and left Claire's ballroom.

Phoebe had watched the exchange with a sinking heart. Claire was in love with the Earl of Wentworth! She was not surprised. She saw Claire fight back tears and instinctively knew they would not see him again. Claire never spoke of it, and Phoebe was afraid to. She grieved for her niece and could do nothing to ease her grief.

The next fortnight passed with invitations to routs, balls, and an expedition to Richmond with a picnic alfresco. Eileen and Lady Jane enjoyed these parties as only the young can. Claire put on her best face and joined in with pleasure, but the memory of Wentworth was never far from her mind.

Nathaniel called one morning early enough to catch her alone. Thinking he looked remarkably fit, Claire welcomed him with pleasure. He always managed to make her look at the events in her life with calm reason. He was a good and trusted friend.

They sat in her small garden and spoke of Eileen's success, and he thanked her for the help she had given them.

"I was at my wit's end when we met that day on the road to London. My life seemed to be over, for I thought I had no prospects. Believe me, I was ready to take a long walk on a short pier."

"Oh, Nate, it was a miracle that we met. You gave us far more than I gave you. Without you I never would have had the opportunity to fulfill a childhood dream. We would have muddled along, and heaven knows what trouble we would have gotten into. And when I suggested my infamous plan, you never said it couldn't be done or even that I should not masquerade as a widow!" Claire replied with a wide smile and shining eyes. "It did work out all for the best. I do not think I would ever be so foolhardy as to take an assumed identity again. We were certainly bold to have done so." She laughed.

"Desperate measures for desperate circumstances, and neither of us had anything to lose. That's the difference," he replied.

"I suppose so, but in hindsight I can hardly credit we did it."

Nate nodded, and a brief silence followed before

he spoke softly. "When I offered for you, I meant it, Claire."

"I know, but it sprang from the circumstances we were in. We were together all the time, but we both know I am not the one for you. You need someone like Lady Jane. I hope you do not let her slip away."

"I don't intend to. I am here for that reason. I am going to offer for her. She will accept me, I think." His smile was so sweet, Claire wanted to reach out and hug him. He was like the brother she never had.

"Oh, Nate, that is wonderful! You are just the right one. They are so empty with the loss of John in battle. You can fill that need. I have seen Lady Jane look at you, and she is head over heels, I tell you."

Nate looked thoughtful. "I am fortunate. I need someone I can take care of. She needs me."

Claire nodded. "I am far too independent. No, Lady Jane is perfect for you."

"I had to come to you before I offered. I did not want you to think I was a fickle heart."

"Nate, I would never think that! I have eyes and can see your growing affection for Lady Jane. I know as well as you that your offer was made out of a sense of chivalry. I know you are devoted to me as I am you, but it is not the kind of love that makes a marriage."

"Yes, but you see why I had to speak to you first. You can depend on me in any way you might need me, Claire. We are family now."

Tears stung Claire's eyes. "Oh, Nate, thank you."

"What of your future?" he asked softly. "London is at your feet. I have seen Peddington and Potts tripping over each other to stand next to you."

Claire laughed. "Yes, I do have a few admirers. There is a mad rumor about that I am plump in the pockets. Such information has a way of enhancing a lady's appeal." Claire's hazel eyes sparkled, and the devilish dimple appeared.

"You are a handsome woman. You have a dozen admirers on your eyes alone and another dozen on your smile."

A cloud slipped across her eyes, and she rose and paced a little. "You're fond of me, Nate. 'Tis natural for you to say so. I fear it is not so for everyone." She sighed.

"Wentworth?"

"Aye."

A silence filled the space between them. Nate took a minute before he replied. "I rather thought he fancied you."

"He does, but for his bed, not his heart."

Tyndall rose. "I'll kill him!"

"Nate, you will do no such thing. I would not have told you had I thought you would take up the gauntlet. He was a gentleman. He asked and I declined—all rather civilized. Fear not, I shall get over him."

Twenty-one

"Phoebe, why don't you want to go to Rosehill with me?" Claire asked at breakfast.

"Dear, it is not Rosehill. I just wish to go to Bath. I liked Bath. Think of all the old ladies for me to play whist with," Phoebe replied, as she added a bit more marmalade on her biscuit.

Claire sighed. "Then, perhaps I, too, should go to Bath."

"As you wish, but please do not do so on my account. Actually, I think it is a bit dull there for you. After all, you are much sought-after here in London. The contrast, I fear, would be too great."

"Hmm . . . I suppose so."

Phoebe watched Claire under her veiled lashes. "You really ought to go to Rosehill and see how the work has gone. The specter of Simon is now gone."

"I do not want to stay in London alone. I feel like everyone is deserting me," Claire said petulantly.

"Now, that is a foolish statement. Nathaniel goes with Lady Jane and Lady Compton to Sterling House in Cotswold. And, of course, he takes Eileen.

I am happy for them all. I never saw a better match. Besides, you were invited, too."

"I know, but I did not want to go. We'll go to the wedding in September, to be sure."

"Of course we will. Back to the subject at hand. I think you should go to Rosehill for the summer. We can decide after Nate and Jane's wedding what we want to do. Surely you're still not harping on Squire Bradley?"

"Aunt Phoebe, I never harp. It is just that . . ."

"The Earl of Wentworth," Phoebe said.

Claire nodded. "Yes, but that aside, I can put a stop to Squire Bradley. Somehow I am sure he will not bother me again."

"You could always write a friendly little letter to the earl," Phoebe said.

"Never! He does not wish a wife."

"I do not think they ever truly do. Hate to give up their freedom," Phoebe added, as though she knew all about men.

Claire sighed again. "I suppose I really should go to Rosehill. I think I shall make it the showplace it once was. That should keep me busy for a year, at least."

"Then go to London for the next Season. Who knows what might happen."

Claire cast her a doubtful look. "Yes, it is home to Rosehill."

"When?"

"When? I do not want to be in London alone. So I shall leave when you do—in a fortnight."

"The summer will do you good. You have looked

a bit wan lately. Now you must excuse me; I have some correspondence to tend to." Phoebe rose and placed a kiss on Claire's forehead. "All will come about, my dear. You'll see."

Claire did not see the smile on Phoebe's face as she bustled out of the room.

Claire kissed Aunt Phoebe good-bye. "I cannot believe we are going our separate ways. I shall miss you!"

"Frankly it's about time we did. You have a life to live, Claire—take the chance." With these cryptic words Phoebe climbed into the coach. Fields and Perkins were up on the box. Claire smiled at Perkins's choice of going to Bath. He said Aunt Phoebe's establishment would have more activity than a manor house stuck in the country.

So O'Mara had been summoned from Rosehill to fetch Claire. He helped Claire and Dora into the traveling coach. Will was to ride outside as protection. Jamie was to follow with the furniture after closing the house.

Claire felt a little sad leaving London. She wondered if she would be back. It had been a wonderful experience. She smiled to herself. She was not the same lady who had left Rosehill a year before. She was grateful for the change. Gone was the ignorant country girl. She was truly her own mistress and confident about the change.

She and Dora exchanged a few words, but for the most part Claire watched the passing landscape in silence. With each mile her spirits rose. England was so lovely. The passing landscape made her realize it would be good to be in the country again for a while. She would take a rod and reel and go fishing at the first opportunity.

It was almost dusk of the second day when they pulled into the Royal Rose. It seemed like a lifetime since she had stayed here. The memory of her silly encounter with Lord Wentworth came to mind. And it *had* been silly. She would never do such a thing again. A little pain stabbed her heart.

Will assisted them out after he had let down the steps. The innkeeper had heard the coach and was on the doorstep with a beaming smile of greeting.

"I have the private dining room at your disposal," he said with a low bow.

Claire lifted an eyebrow. My, she thought, could he remember her from so long ago? He seemed to be expecting her. Dora headed up the stairs to their room, behind the innkeeper's wife, and Will brought up the rear with the hatbox and valise.

Claire entered the dining room. The Earl of Wentworth stood by the window and turned at her entrance.

"My Lord Wentworth!"

"Good evening, Mrs. Anseley. Welcome. I have been waiting for you. Two days, actually. Innkeeper, some sherry, please. Mrs. Anseley looks faint."

Claire's first inclination was to flee, but her steps carried her into the room.

Her heart leapt with the joy of seeing him. He

looked as handsome as ever in riding clothes and shiny Hessians. His eyes were intent on her.

"What are you doing here?" she asked.

"Waiting for you."

"Waiting for me? I do not understand. How could you know I was coming here?"

"Aunt Phoebe, your dear, darling Aunt Phoebe. It seems I have a supporter in her."

Claire's mouth fell open. "I don't believe you. She would not betray me."

"Perhaps it is not a betrayal. Then, of course, there is O'Mara." He smiled at her, and the tenderness in his eyes was unmistakable.

"O'Mara? He is your man?"

Wentworth nodded.

"You are beyond presumptuous!"

"Beyond redemption," he said, and took a step toward her. "It is good to see you, Claire. You have never been out of my thoughts."

Just then the innkeeper entered, carrying a tray with a decanter of sherry and two glasses. He set it on the table and slipped quietly from the room.

Wentworth took up the decanter and poured a glass. "My dear Mrs. Anseley, you look a little pale. Sit down, please." He handed her the glass.

In a daze Claire obeyed. She took a chair, to the relief of her wobbly legs. The sip of wine warmed her throat and stilled her fluttering stomach.

"I cannot credit you have been doing all this!"

He ignored her remark. "How have you been, Claire?"

"I have managed to exist."

197

"Then you have fared far better than I."

She looked up at him but made no reply.

"Claire, I have been miserable without you."

"You will forgive me if I remind you that it was all your choice."

"I know, that is the worst part. I alone spoiled what we might have had. Can you forgive me?"

"I did so already." She lifted her chin and looked him in the eyes.

She rose and placed her glass on the table. "It is not seemly for me to be alone with you in an inn."

"Claire, grant me the time to plead my case."

"No, you have been given my answer."

"I shall go down on bended knee, my love, if you wish. I cannot live without you. Marry me, Claire."

She stopped and turned.

He stepped forward. "I know I should have asked ages ago. Probably in this very courtyard when I rescued you from certain death under the horse hooves! That surely needs some consideration."

Claire smiled. "But you had just met me then."

"Exactly my point. I held you once and lost my heart. I cannot believe I let you slip away. You are all I ever hoped for in a woman. It is said that once a man saves another's life, he is responsible for that person forever. You would not deny me my honor, surely."

"You are ruthless."

"Totally. Besides, Julie needs you. Think of the dear child—without a mother. She asks about you all the time. I even told her I would bring you back to Dublin."

"You stop at nothing."

"Nothing."

"Your own daughter?"

"Yes, she is my trump card. She needs a mother, and you would be the perfect candidate."

"You would use your daughter as a ploy?" Claire smiled.

"All's fair in love and war. The end justifies the means. Any port in a storm. He who hesitates is lost. And, besides, I love you!"

She was in his arms before she knew it. He held her so close, she could hardly breathe. "Claire, never be more than a room away for the rest of my life."

He kissed her lips, her cheeks, her eyes, and her hair, and began again.

"Wentworth, you are impossible! I shall probably regret this for the rest of my life, but I give you an unequivocal yes!"

He kissed her again and again, whispering all the silly things lovers are wont to say and that sound utterly ridiculous to others not afflicted by that reducing sentiment.

Finally he pulled apart. His jade eyes smoldered with the fire of his kisses and her loving response. He reached into his pocket and produced a folded parchment.

"This is a special license, my love, and I have the local vicar waiting in the other room. Dora and Will can be our witnesses. Marry me now. This moment. I am afraid to give you time to think it over."

"A vicar waiting? A special license? You are rather sure of yourself."

"On the contrary, I am scared to death. I was afraid you would reject me outright. I don't want you to think it over," he said, and laughed. He pulled her back into his arms.

And so the Earl and Countess of Wentworth were married in an inn on the road from London on an early summer's evening. When they entered the bedchamber (the same one Claire had commandeered a year before), his lordship made an observation.

"You know, of course, that I married you so as to sleep in this chamber rather than be foisted out into a wee room down the hall."

Claire feigned surprise. "You married me for a larger bedroom? Squire Bradley only wanted my land."

"There's no accounting for taste. Now, my love, keep in mind I had to marry you in order to get you for my mistress. You strike a hard bargain."

"Yes, and you just remember that the rest of our lives." She placed her arms around his neck.

"Claire, I just had a startling notion. I have been giving myself credit for capturing you! Suddenly I am wondering if it is I caught in *your* web! Hmm, no matter. This is where I want to be."

He untied her bonnet and placed it on the dresser. "Claire, I love you." His kiss would be remembered a lifetime.

More Romance from Regency